On the Winding Stair

On the Winding Stair

—m—

By Joanna Howard

AMERICAN READER SERIES, NO. 12

BOA EDITIONS, LTD. —m— ROCHESTER, NY —m— 2009

First Edition
09 10 11 12 7 6 5 4 3 2 1

For information about permission to reuse any material from this book please contact The Permissions Company at www.permissionscompany.com or e-mail permdude@eclipse. net.

Publications by BOA Editions, Ltd. – a not-for-profit corporation under section 501 (c) (3) of the United States Internal Revenue Code – are made possible with funds from a variety of sources, including public funds from the New York State Council on the Arts, a state agency; the Literature Program of the National Endowment for the Arts; the County of Monroe, NY; the Lannan Foundation for support of the Lannan Translations Selection Series; the Sonia Raiziss Giop Charitable Foundation; the Mary S. Mulligan Charitable Trust; the Rochester Area Community Foundation; the Arts & Cultural Council for Greater Rochester; the Steeple-Jack Fund; the Ames-Amzalak Memorial Trust in memory of Henry Ames, Semon Amzalak and Dan Amzalak; and contributions from many individuals nationwide.

See Colophon on page 128 for special individual acknowledgements.

Cover Design: Sandy Knight
Cover Art: Rikki Ducornet
Interior Design and Composition: Bill Jones
Manufacturing: BookMobile
BOA Logo: Mirko

Library of Congress Cataloging-in-Publication Data

Howard, Joanna, 1975-
On the winding stair / by Joanna Howard. -- 1st ed.
    p.cm. – (American reader series no. 12)
ISBN 978-1-934414-25-5 (alk. paper)
I. Title

PS3608.O924O6 2009
813'.6--dc22

                              2009006721

NATIONAL
ENDOWMENT
FOR THE ARTS
A great nation
deserves great art.

BOA Editions, Ltd.
Nora A. Jones, Executive Director/Publisher
Thom Ward, Editor/Production
Peter Conners, Editor/Marketing
Bernadette Catalana, BOA Board Chair
A. Poulin, Jr., Founder (1938-1996)
250 North Goodman Street, Suite 306
Rochester, NY 14607
www.boaeditions.org

State of the Arts

NYSCA

for Brian

Table of Contents

On the winding stair
Your dress rustles.

Candle burning quietly
In the dark room—
A silver hand
Snuffs it out.

—Georg Trakl (translated by Keith Waldrop)

Light Carried on Air Moves Less

In a lavender twilight, on the west side of an abandoned pasture gone to hay in the greenest part of our state, a mendicant: a scarved pale beauty with silver bell earrings, curled to sleep on kinked metal filings on the floor of a windowless farm shed gone to rot. In the center of that plain, where parched pasture grass muled, low and reedy, and sucked the humid thickness from the air till it was pinched and light and porous, a loose-ended portion of train track sat on its chalky rock pile, plank ribbed, veined with dark steel rails. This night, as on every night for a very long time with no pink left in the sky, a knobby russet handcar ratcheted its way across the excerpt of track, up the length, back and up again, with imperceptibly audible chirps, its pilot a thin, lit specter almost entirely in bed dress. This specter was only slightly opaque in the darkness and so narrow that his striped muffler was wrapped around his neck several times, so that the thick, frazzled mound of it seemed to balance his white wisped head and hold it upright. He cranked the handle of the Irish mail handcar and his motion was so slow not even the nightshirt's misty tails wafted behind him as he slumped weakly from ennui. That night, he was not seen by the wandering beauty who was too sleepy to notice his glowing plod, and who, instead, bundled herself into her scarves and slept, a gauzy crinkled lump of blues and pinks, faintly heaving and tinkling from within.

The beauty slept through the morning and woke up musky in her ball of sweat-soaked scarves and brushed away light metal curls. On bare and filthy soles, she walked into the pasture, a prismatic windblown form not unlike a specter of a more colorful variety, one which might not normally occur to us, and in the pasture she saw the handcar and examined it, spoked and rusted and mammoth, like some great, weathered clockworks. Clung to the handcar ratchet, the specter, with knobbed kneecaps, examined the pale beauty whose scarves glinted with metallic threads and who smelled somewhat fermented to someone who had smelled only the ground-up rust-mist of the creaking ratchet tines for a long time. Or at least she smelled entirely unlike the specter, who smelled to himself like not really anything. And there was the sound of her earrings, battered and tangled in waving, greasy hair mats, clicking arhythmically, which filled the specter with a sense of renewed purpose. When she rounded the left-most rear wheel and drug a gritty nail over a rusted spoke, he pouted dramatically, but imperceptibly, not luminous in the sunlight, not even as much as reflective.

The beauty stared beyond him, a long way even on a plain as flat as this was, and for the first time noticed the wind gale and, unfettered, unassuming, pledged her love and faithfulness to the wind in a loud, lispy wail, which the specter of course confused as a direct address. He did his best to imitate his idea of a ghosty sob, which sounded more like an allergic sniff, the faint pop of which had no effect on the beauty who instead wandered beyond the handcar and deeper into the pasture.

In addition to a rotting, but well-roofed, farm shed, the abandoned pasture had a gray and flaky farmhouse with no roof at all and one side missing, gone entirely from sight, like a cutaway dollhouse. Overtaken by melon-blossomed trumpet vine and long spindly shoots of rose of Sharon, the three remaining walls of that open parlor left deep gray shadows in the declining sun, and the vines curled under and around the legs and arms of a mossy settee and bound it in place against the western wall.

Inevitably, when the afternoon had gotten as hot as it could get in even this green part of our state, the impoverished beauty wandered out of the pasture and left the specter to sulk, fingering his woolly muffler fringe, until sundown. The beauty stepped onto the foundation of the farmhouse and turned back to face the wind which entered and eddied in the tableau parlor, and she looked out at the pasture reverent with bent pasture grass and a hardly notable handcar.

The pale beauty felt a burble in her stomach and ran a palm down her belly which was round only with scarves.

She turned to the western wall and picked through a curtain of trumpet vine to a hallway and into a remnant of kitchen. In the kitchen she found a pantry filled with shelves of wax-sealed canning jars filled with fig paste, bonneted in minty gingham and darkly iridescent, purply-green through their glass walls. Shoveling with crooked fingers, the pale beauty packed her cheeks and jaw with sticky fig paste, smacked, and gobbed for all she was worth.

On the floor of the pantry, in a moist corner shaded by canning shelves, a swollen, yellowed tome, *Pauline's Life of a Madam*, lay molding and untouched. The beauty hefted it, still holding her fig paste jar and flipped open its cover. Inside, in large block print for the seeing impaired, were stories of fancy women, cabaret girls, saloon floozies and peepshow demoiselles, all tawdry and fecund and richly illustrated with tri-color drawings: black outlined bosomy scanty-clads, yellow and pink and pale blue in pantaloons, loose-laced corsets, feathery merry-widows, all of them spilling forth, pouring forth, top-heavy in sketched-up décolletage.

The pale beauty lugged the book into her elbow crook, made her way down the hall to her windy, terraced parlor and collapsed on the vined settee swirling with the tiny red specks of spider mites. She lapped fig and read out loud to the wind, till she wasn't conscious of doing either and fell asleep with the last streaks of pink still hanging, determined, above her western wall.

In the pasture, now glowing hazily, the specter bent to his handcar handle, sniffed into his muffler, and eked up the track with lax shirttails, somewhat jilted, and tried to work up a friction between ghosty tongue and ghosty teeth. He could sense nothing happening.

The morning sun spot-lit the beauty's sleeping stage and she stretched out scarf-silken wing-crepe, lamé specked and sparkling, and smiled to the wind, which this day was absent, everything still as the rustbound handcar and not prairielike in its usual way. With no wind to speak of, she slumped on the open side of her parlor, dangled feet off the floor's edge and licked at fig-sweet fingers. The specter, though he was a great distance away, was used to peeking through dark space and so squinted and strained to watch the beauty who seemed as bright as a coupling of fairies, which the specter didn't believe in, with good reason.

She soon dragged her book onto her lap and read into the afternoon, waiting for the wind, which did not so much as waft, leaving her earrings dull and silent.

She waited what seemed to her a very long time. She stood, outstretched scarf-looped arms, wished for some moment of flapping, some metaled whistle in her ears, and she examined herself and thought of the book, open now to a drawing of a pinky can-can girl, petticoats heaped at her ankles, striped stockings strung loose from garters, and for a moment, she thought she had something figured out.

In the hallway closet, whose floor was split through with juniper shrub, the beauty found the tattered remains of a tapestry sewing box which she hauled out of prickly branches. The box was filled with ribbings and edgings, snarled yarn balls and half-pieced quilt swatches, a large portion of unraveling coffee-table doily. With only the top-most layer of scarves, she darned and lashed together the roughest equivalent of a century-old chemise in navy and rose, edged in loose strung doily scallops. She finished as the sun was just descending, and folded the tiny creation into a small square and tucked it into the sewing box and buried it in vines under the settee.

The specter, as he prepared for his motion up the tracks, concentrated his attention on the drowsy eyes of the beauty reclined on her couch of vines and tried to glow more than at any other time in his afterlife, and thought, for a moment, that he was the most phosphorescent, the most luminous. Maybe he was faintly more brilliant for all his desire, but light carried on air moves less on windless nights, and to anyone watching he might have seemed dimmer than ever before.

When the sun rose the next morning behind the specter's dissipating spine, the beauty unfurled her scarved arms, poked bare toe tips beyond the fluttery points of loose scarf garb, laggard, stretched spiny shins, and unbent sleep-stoved knees. She stood at the edge of her parlor, cupped filthy fingers over eyebrows, and stared into the still pasture, beyond the unmoving, unvascilate pasture grass, well beyond the unnotable Irish mail with its insubstantial, passion-sick wraith, almost as though she could see all the way to the point where the wind began, when it began, which it had not this day. And in the still watchfulness of the pasture, the watchfulness of a perpetually insomniac specter, she asked for the wind. With the stamping of tiny, leather-bottomed feet she began to cast off scarves, jerked with tight, pinched fingers, in long ribbony banners of lavender blue, fuscia, blood blue, midnight blue, robin's egg, carmine, sangria, black blue, mauve, until she stood a pale knobby creature, more like a specter than anything else, in fact like nothing else in the world other than a specter, or so thought our slope-backed handcar captive who became so short of soundless breath that he clawed at his muffler coil till his transparent throat windowed with sunlight.

In a moment she was hunched down, fishing and cloying in the settee vines, and she dragged out the tapestried sewing kit where, carefully stowed inside, was the handcraft from the previous afternoon which she slipped loosely into and which hooped her dust-marked thighs, and swayed with dripping doily tatter. On the floor, she pressed back the stiff cover pieces of *Pauline's Life of a Madam* and posed in a way that was just similar enough to the bawdy line-drawing to suggest a deliberate imitation, hands on wide-spread knees, upturned east-facing tailbone, an attempted over-the-shoulder glance of provocative understanding, tongue unfurled, winking. She held this posture for several minutes with yogic determination. Then, returned to the book, flipped a stiff warped page and repositioned, foot propped on settee, left hand on waist-hip curve, right arm stretched out, a curling index finger to the east. She continued this stilted peepshow dance, turned pages, each posture increasing in lewdness and awkward displays of fleeting equilibrium, and she waited for the wind which did not so much as puff up the corners of discarded, earthbound scarves.

Through all this, the specter watched, and with each new posture felt a level of death that he was sure marked the most dead moment of his afterlife, and he sensed an unhealthy vibration about his transparent parameters and wondered if it was possible for a ghost to combust to light and ash from sheer will, just for the sake of being finally seen.

The afternoon waned to a thin coral haze, a bank of unmoving clouds and the production continued squats, kicks, splay-legged pliés, an unsuccessful full-tilt back-bend, and all of it, sans wind, until the deep lavender precursor to haunting was in its last moments and the specter felt he was coming, decidedly, to the end of some damn thing.

The beauty, however, did not collapse on her bed of vines, but rather increased her range of motion and rapidity of postures, so enraptured in her performance that she failed to note the eerie pathetic aura of the handcar, and its slight, strained first rolls.

Though she grew dim on her darkened parlor stage, it did not discourage the specter's desire, but made it all the more unbearable, and he thought for a moment that this could only go on, and it could go on, for days or weeks in a drought of wind indifferent to the wishes of beggars or ghosts. And with this thought and a palpable sense of dread which he could only describe as lumpy and earth-like he began to pump all the harder on his handcar crank crunching up the rails and back with an increasing but un-noticed cacophony until not only his shirttails were flapping behind him but a sparkling eddy of air and motion swirled out around him.

The motion built to an elaborate fantastical cyclonic whirl which picked up the ensemble of scarves in a swirling, brilliant funnel, which flattened and severed soft unsuspecting pasture grasses, and which picked up the hair of the pale beauty, tore away the garish and delicate chemise and in a last fitful tug, scooped up the long white body whose momentary rapture was focused on the vibrant earthly manifestation of a wind so powerful it could move rust-bound handcars on weed-lashed tracks, so powerful it could make a storm of scarves obscuring the moon, powerful enough to grant the wishes of pale, hungry girls.

In the wind-spun eye of the handcar storm, for the specter there was only this: the thin clicked chime of ever ascending silver baubles, and a motion so heavy and constant it was like sitting still.

—∞—

Captive Girl for Cobbled Horsemen

From the ditch below the family graves, where she huddled softly in the shadow of a stone, the small child was taken up into a new community. A transition toward different civility followed roughly across several years: a new weave of fabric, daughter or wife, a vengeful scar across the right cheek of her captor, thread made from sinews, ever so many dogs crossing and recrossing the mobile compound and surveying the parameters.

And of those left behind her? On a deathbed, the last fading matriarch cobbles a makeshift family from extensions and tatters: a wild boy pulled from the cactus, a deserter cavalry man riding trick on some horses, and the fugitive uncle suspected of murder. These are the riches on earth left to a little girl kept captive in one compound, far from the safety of another compound, and far from that last passageway before death! And so the search continues, at the hands of a new collective.

Some dark time passes, and the girl removed, continues removed, remiss. Her garments turn up for trade. A new head of hair comes on to her in curls. There is little sleep in the compound, for the baying dogs, for the scouts left edging along the pickets, for the girl sharing only so much of a corner with several other girls. Exhaustion builds, sockets darken and sink, so much of her face grows beyond her child's mouth. They move on together, nomadic, and self-sufficient. In the distance, some vague pursuant.

On the edge of the river and the border between countries, a ranch sprung up rather from the dust of nothing stands idle and anticipating. It is a stationary compound, shaped, after a given time, according to the times, for a family who welcomed the hardship of hard ground, where the high plains surrounded smokily, red and exposed. Four structures briefly crenellate the horizon: a cylindrical water tower rising above a deep round of troughs, a crisp white farm house edging onto the corrals, the barn, the maid's quarters.

In this abandoned farm house, in the shadowed corner of a pale room, a bed awaits the returning girl who, polished and hushed of fears, might take up where things were left off. But how were they left off, and who is left to take up? As the years pass, quite quickly in fact, she floats apart from the dream of the bed, and the memory of someone stooped gently above it. There had only been one brother after the war, and then, somehow, another campaign followed. Are any brothers left? Any mothers?

In their travels, the red dirt becomes sand, and the sand gives way to salt, and the west drifts blankly, and blindingly, before them. Another camp built and picketed at the foot of the mountains.

Over the campfire two men begin a transaction, but a satisfactory agreement cannot be struck. He catches her in the corner of his eye, passing obliquely between dogs. Much later, as he leaves their compound, two scouts polish their weapons, but are not seen again. Several days pass, without event, in the sweltering white.

On evenings, she wanders in the hills to search for clay mud to carry back in the flat of a basket. In a white cave, with water slipping along the lime, she discovers the torn sleeve of a man's shirt. She recognizes the fabric, blood-soaked and homespun, and she tucks it up into her dress to be fit later quite naturally into an emerging puzzle.

From here she descends, and so the two parties meet finally just below the shelf of the mountain. Down in the white valley, the skirmishes have already begun, along a thin bed of water cupped in the curve of the drifting flat. Even here, salt infects the pool. Now the pursuer takes lead, on horseback, at the head of the procession, a narrow line obscured in the rising dust. In the distance at high gallop, the cavalry man rides standing up across two horses. The boy from the cactus grown now to the height of a great, dark man slips barefoot from his saddleless horse toward her, imploring, she imagines, to slit her throat. And so begins her roughshod removal.

But what grand cobblings await her: his broad back, his horseman's hands, his slow drawl, his grim stagger, his soft step, his dark eyes, the white arm soon to be removed, grinning blackly below the torn seam of the shoulder. Oh my uncles, my brothers, fresh from memory come to take me home!

Severed and refitted, she now begins the flight to this strange future from this imagined past.

—∿—

Exchange

The glass lantern is fractured. It's time to start slowly.

She wore a cloisonné earring in the shape of a fish. Harry James was playing on the Victrola. He spoke at the bar, softly, so as not to interrupt. The gentleman across from him was a confused type.

My mother and father were brother and sister, the gentleman told him.

He agreed and excused himself.

She slipped about the room like walking on petals on pillows on air. He approached her.

Please, she said. I'm guilty enough just standing here.

He had his answer, and still it seemed he'd heard the song before.

—∞—

The Black Cat

I.

In unseasonable torrents, the car overturns on the road at the foot of a long curling driveway, the chauffeur's head crushed against the glass. The passengers are unscathed. Thank God, says the American. Of course, now your honeymoon is ruined, says the Hungarian aristocrat. The American looks at the fainting woman in his arms. Well, it's not like that, he tells him, that would be too, too much.

In the hilltop mansion, the bell rings Rachmaninoff. Behind the poster bed's veil, the elemental doctor rises to touch the forehead of his child bride. The hand he passes over her eyes deepens her coma. Stay in bed tomorrow, he tells her, don't tax yourself, darling.

In the foyer, the American blows a low whistle. This place is swank, he tells the Hungarian. It's Deco, the Hungarian corrects, we've got that here, too. The bright high doors pop open with the pressure of a finger on the gilt crossbar. The black cat emerges. The frightened Hungarian shuttles a small dagger at the animal, deftly pinning a front paw to the carpet. Now see here, announces the American.

I, in my crystal box, await the return of my husband from the war.

II.

By then the rain is slowed and stopped. The Mongolian valet cradles the platinum damsel. His mustache is a waxy fake. The path twists up the hill, a mile at a turn. The air holds the storm's cymbal, its precipitous brunt, but the sky lights clear and cloudless.

Soon she will be walking. She couldn't help the thought of some strange fingers shifting about in her hair as she slept in the railcar, the nails sharply bronzed. In the halls of the great architect, in her effortless gauze drape, she will enter his library like sliding on ice. The bright solid patch of a bandage, discernible under the chandelier's glare, emerges from beneath her ruffled organza.

Her eyes are thick, her gestures mute. Do I need more dressing? she asks the writer, perched on the arm of the wing chair. And how, my sweet. Can someone get her an iced tea? he announces to the host. The architect is distracted, already the cogwheels grind. I'm sure the necessary drugs have been administered, he tells his guest. The effect, as you must know, is always unpredictable.

I'm left with a great deal of questions, the damsel tells her audience, with measured phrasing. Here the black cat begins her third ascent, from death, from the seamless travertine.

Her senses either blotted or more acute.

III.

Behind the Japanese screen the two great men are alone in silhouette. My trip has been long and arduous, the Hungarian declares.

They say that wars change men, the architect tells him.

That is what they say, but then I have never been one of those kind of soldiers.

I might have guessed as much.

Between these two, some manner of business remains uncovered. They step so lightly on paws, their shadows cross and merge. And what if the question remains unasked: What have you done with Karin?

I am trying to collect some pieces, the Hungarian reminds his host. In my mind, I recall two faces.

One came sooner and one much later.

Had I a daughter?—I'd forgotten. The earlier picture is the one that interests me.

Dead.

And the latter?

Dead as well.

And did they look quite perfectly alike?

That is often the way things go.

I am tempted to thank you for your kindness, Hjalmar, especially if this is all there is to it.

Vetus, we both know that below any great mansion lies a larger, greater mansion.

Often so.

The Hungarian hums low to demonstrate a certain doubt. There must always be something so tangible between things.

IV.

In the library, misgiving huddles in the stacks. Again her frills are bristling. The electric candelabra portends a crushing blow from overhead. Her skin glows with crystalline powder.

I slipped out of bed, she tells the gentlemen, cigars smoldering beside the trunks of their snifters. Too much satin, she shrugs.

She's a real deuce, the writer announces. Always yucking it up. But while I beg your entire pardon, I can't help wondering, is this the way it should go?

The hush from the ranks is stiffening. They hang on her next phrase, every line farsighted. She lingers angularly adrift. The smile is pleasant at best.

V.

Beyond the peaked windows the dark is firmly settled. No one can guess the hour. The sky awaits a ritual moon. The party, with agitated senses, disperses to the chambers, the staircase a long curling spiral to the third floor.

The Hungarian in his room lays out monogrammed pajamas and a quilted jacket. The writer peels back the accordion divider to light the bed silk. His marcelling is starting to give: one waxy tendril has dropped over his left eye. Backlit, he wears a different age. I can't help but feel safe, he announces. In that case, we ought to switch, the doctor suggests.

For the writer, exhaustion mounts around the eyes. He tucks hands in pockets and offers a rough shrug. I'm starting to feel a bit out of the dynamic, he tells the doctor, who offers a nod of support. Actually he's coming into his own. Seraphic and haggard, like something brought in, he's developed a slight appeal.

The writer twists at the knees. I wasn't cast to play the rake.

No, of course, the Hungarian tells him, but all our parts are shifting.

VI.

At the mansion's center, stairs curl up four flights in a perfect cylinder, and the tube that remains unfilled illuminates a spot on the marble from the skylight above. A table has been brought out and dressed for playing. All at once the chess game has begun; the players seated on velvet cushions stretch long legs out from the marble table. The winner will select the sacrifice.

The two young lovers are clad in tweed for travel. The blonde's eyes are smoky and clotted. I don't think I'll ever get a wink in this dump, she tells the writer. It's time to hotfoot it.

Are you vastly improved? the doctor asks her. Her tongue and lips remain thickly numbed. Whose side are you on anyway?

Things are hotting up nicely, the doctor tells his opponent. I haven't played in years, but I can't image I'll lose.

That's the kind of thing I hear a lot, says the architect.

Ciao, the lovers are saying as they slowly step backwards out of the circle. Ciao and thanks heap-loads; they wave at the gentlemen.

In the shadows, the tapestry pattern obscures a hulking figure. The Turkish henchman cracks his knuckles. His arms extend into the light.

VII.

Under the house, a fortress ruin is situated, stairwells and corridors curving down into the crust. In the very pit the séance begins, the gentry stacked thick in lamé sheaths and dinner jackets. The Occultist reads softly from a satanic text, the folds of his kimono gaping black.

The sacrificial altar lines up the chiasmic portrait. The virgin is running late; her hair is being done at a skirted vanity, several floors up, inside the house. I am the very essence of the part, she tells the servant. Look at this bracelet, it really shines indoors. But you and I know it's how it looks in the sun that counts.

The Occultist looks thin inside his robes; he seats himself roughly on the edge of the makeshift stage. The audience, impatient for a sacrifice, yawns, sipping from flasks. Once a leader always a leader, the Hungarian tells our host, and takes his hand. Finally, he says, I am of two minds on you.

I'm sorry for that, Vetus. All I want to say is how tiring it all gets. Yes, the Hungarian admits, that is certainly the case with any profession.

Already the panels of the walls are shifting as the Hungarian strokes those long gray fingers. He hopes for the courage to cut the skin from the bones.

VIII.

A cellar vault must turn around to align the open doors. So much depends on technology in these ancient systems. The writer may be lucky to break out of his prison, but with each passing hour he puts on character like so many winter clothes. The nature of these stories is that something must give. He is building up a certain charge, and awaiting the release.

This is the level at the very bottom of it all, gouged out of several layers of rock. The mansion above is well insulated; with every room comes a fire glowing out of frame. It might be nice to find the room up there with an inviting corner trap to crumple in. No doubt there are many, but complaints will get you nowhere. The air here is cool enough to keep us looking our best. A fur coat is tempting, but ultimately not advisable. Where will a cat-suit get you these days? Sleep is the key, though my daughter's is periodically broken.

This is the moment when someone should comment on how things hang in the balance. As with a picture, they should not be encouraged to tilt too much. I remain within my glass shelter. In the end, these walls might be razed in strips, like peeling fruit, or they might come down in shards.

—⁂—

Seascape

In the haunted cottage by the sea, I settled into the seaman's berth. The captain was long since dead from his own hand. I came from the west in widow's garb with a trousseau in cedar. Drawn to the sea, again. The sea which captivates men with motherly arms and swimming dark womb is no place for a lady.

In the beginning I only heard laughing. His portrait in brooding oils hung in every room. The balcony's French doors swung open of their own accord. I had been very lonely for a very long time. Below the bedroom's balcony, dark waters spilled into a narrow cove. The deck chairs, clothed in damp canvas, faced seaward on their precarious stage. Through nights I kept watch. Shadows and flashes in the movement of the night waters. Nightmares disband in sweet lingering insomnia. I was very good at looking straight ahead.

In time we lulled each other. He crept out of his painting and moved among his own things. The rooms doubled their size. The house shifted carefully, and the air inside grew thick and pendulous, and the furniture swelled near to bursting. Nothing was mine, but was done up according to demand in scrimshaw and leather, blue velveteen, and papered walls. I preferred the traditional black, though all of my under-clothes were convent-made in silk and lace. I undressed behind a painted screen, and felt a slight breath—certainly feigned—on my shoulder. We had not yet been introduced.

I was getting lovelier in the days that followed. Men in two-seater cars drove up the hill and down again. I took no suitors. Another courtship had begun. In our bedroom, his figure slipped out from the shadows and hardened its form, square and unshaven. He appeared as though he might speak. Here began the affectation of the living: breath, glance, speech from the mouth. Sounds came rough and un-sorted. I fell deeply asleep, and in my dreams the sea air and its vapors, gaining force, stirred the bed clothes, and I awoke bathed.

The memory becomes very sweet, and the hands of the clock spin forward. Most days, he came and disturbed the contents of the room. His voice drew together in scraps and curses, and with it a certain perspective. I attempted to re-cord his advances. He held together in a dashing form, and his sweater buttoned at the shoulder. Now, gaining voice, he had quite a lot to add. I accustomed myself to an unvar-nished point of view. Language which meant all too clearly what it said. Periodically, his name burst with violence into the air, which I repeated to myself in a whisper, removed away to the darkness of the closet. Even there I was well accompanied. I was plunged into community. In the late afternoon, the fog came down from the cliffs, and settled in so close around the house it blocked even the view of the balcony's rail from the lounge where I sat, most often, near to fainting. It brought him in close as well, out of the haze, and, fluid and silent, he knelt at my elbow. There was no time to be lost in admiring him.

Though his temper was cooling I felt, if not quite wanted, that I was waiting in line. Outside, the short lawn collected a periphery of spectators. Three bombshell silhouettes in ragged black crepe slipped up among the beach grass, watchful and distrusting. The captain refused to comment. In modern times, I might have had competition, but ours was an arranged affair.

Some years passed, and the road lay still and broken with weeds. An auburn hound, with feral eyes, followed me through the house and slept at my feet. I draped my shoulders in tartan. I spoke often and in all directions to a captive audience. In wakeful hours, with the light high over the water, I waited for the night that disrobes. A certain fear crossed my mind. How long before the past, in finally forgiving, would open up and give him passage? It was enough for me to live at the water's edge, on the spirits' line, and wait to be over–taken.

I woke and slept. In sleep's reverie, taking his arm, I found it opaque and firm. We walked up the steep incline from the beach to the cottage. We began together in step, my wild dog held close. Moving along the path, the captain was at our height, and then moving apart from us, far ahead and above. The air wavered, and I dropped into fever.

That day, the sky and the sea met at a narrow seam. Like the hinge in a dream which, closing, changes the register. The room kept silent. Beyond the French doors, the horizon held steady. All I could see was what I could see.

I cast about inside the house, held as I was to the hope of his return. In this way, I haunted. I catalogued my memories and counted among them several of his that had passed between us. I might have thought it unlike a thing to possess in itself a soul and a memory. Years passed, but I kept current in the blush of love.

I married the place. This was the more lasting of the two liaisons. Loving so solitary a horizon, when one has been abandoned, proves some compensation for absence. If a lesson follows, then don't look for truth in dark waters. The thin scrim of my captain's cottage kept all picture windows facing seaward, and so, in passing from glass to glass, I followed that unchanging vista, a reminder of the one who never abandons.

—⁓—

Russian Doll

Small eyes: the puffed, white lids of distended sockets and their veiny balls in translucent coating, whitened irises, smooth glowing pupils. Lips: pale; brackenish unraveling sweater: pale; curling red-beard gone faint, cheeks faint, hair faintly greased and reflective. In an irrigation canal of a half-flooded cornfield, several inches of a man hovers above the murky surface, all gone quite dim. A large drowned man is bobbing, delicately, like an undulating mound, a water-logged paunch arcing out of the water. His head brushes against the cement support wall of the canal, below a foot-bridge. A very spongy sound, as the water cuts under the footbridge of a road dividing corn from sorghum.

A man has drowned in a canal in a cornfield, a high-walled, glorified ditch, belonging not only to a cornfield, but a sorghum field, and from the footbridge he can only be seen fully when leaning over the edge, for instance: stand-ing on the lowest rung of the footbridge's slatted side-wall, sneaker soles curving over the board for balance, belly flattened against the middle slat, top slat tucked under the arms, cutting into the breastplate. Were someone looking for a beaver, say, a small dam had been erected a mile down the canal and noticed on a walk with the dogs—before all these rains. And if that same one—his or her dogs now curled on rank, flannel mats wanting no part of the cool air of the suspended storms, chilled humidity rising off the standing floodwater—positioned on the footbridge were to curl the toes over the first rung, arms over the top rung, etc., and glimpse a pale flash of greasy hair, hear that sound, brushing the wall of the canal. A beaver? The water has come up the sides of the canal, almost level with the road, already rising waist high in the field, and a drowned man is floating below the bridge in a murky, but mostly pale sweater, staring with white eyes skyward.

But it is hard to tell where the canal stops and the field begins. Flooding has submerged the sorghum completely, and the rusty floe is up to the tassels on the corn which sits in the valley of the field, up mid-stalk on the hilltop. In some places it's soaking the road. Only the footbridge is completely dry, even as it is, hanging slightly over the drowned man, whose left arm extended overhead, unreasonably positioned, has caught his sleeve on something in the space just below the boards, hard to say what, from this angle.

Debris, once-living, now dull and bloated: A drowned man has worked his way into a canal, as things are wont to do. Moreover, you note, a drowned man has worked himself into a flooded field where, overnight, crops are yellowing and weeping downward, like, like suicides, and this is one more in a series of drowned things, strangely rooted and wafting despite themselves.

—∞—

What Was There Was Gone, Burning

In November the bullets shattered the dining room window glass, cut past brocade curtains, one at a time, and put each of our great-uncles down in an orderly fashion, through a shoulder of the first, the arm of the other, the left side temple of the first, square in the back of the other, till they were slumping, red-marked masses.

Outside the dismantled fairgrounds, we buried their bodies, wiping away the last spots of tomatoes Creole from their beards. We spaded the half-rigored bodies of our two great-uncles into trackside ditches of sumac, our forearms ridged at first with the colorless rash of the leaf poison, then slowly deepening red, in streaks, traveling upwards to our elbows as we chopped through the surface roots of the trees. I kicked down the shallow mound, marking the rise with boot-heel half moons. We both raised feet and stamped down a grave, a heavy working against rhythm of girls in too-large boots. My sister had taken Earl's from the fireplace, and mine were Loba's. But it was Loba who Gayla looked down at through the dark rust of sumac, through a thin layer of Ozark mud and root, through pale lids sealed against it. And it was as though she were asking him if he was good there, if she'd done it all right. The double hemmed wool edge of her skirt had stiffened with blood, and she steadied herself on the splintered rod of her shovel as she climbed up the slope to the train rail where I waited.

It was then that I remembered, almost realized again, what I much later told Gayla had been an accident, an intervention of God: the pot of water I'd left howling on the stovetop as we wrapped their bony frames in torn parts of Aunt Elva's crocheted table cloth and dragged, sloppily, the then clotting bodies from their supper chairs over Aunt Ivo's false Persian rugs. We left stone cups of rosehips, ginger powder and crisp black tea leaves upturned in the carpet's fringe.

Now, we'd buried them. We'd pulled them in their cloths through a field behind the house, along the tracks behind the fairgrounds, and our great-aunts with dumb mouths moved slowly behind us. Their arms were locked, their dark coats swinging. And I'd sent them up the track into the woods to wait for us, to save them the look of our expressions as we cut through the ditch roots. And after, we moved up the track, our shovels at our sides. We didn't know what to do with them but drag them, scraping in the gravel, bumping on each ridged tie.

We moved up the train tracks, farther still past the empty mud circles of the fairgrounds, and into the outer woods, under the weeping overhang of mistletoe clotted in the joints of spare-leaved elms. We moved till the narrow black of the Tar Creek railbridge was tall in front of us and we crossed down into the creek bed where the two great-aunts sat huddled beside each other in the catnip and crabgrass of the slope. Below the first beam of the trestle, they sat in over-sized wool pea coats so long they wrapped their ankles and cast shadows over high-buttoned shoes. They held a black paste-board book of photographs they'd dragged from the house. On the page: cut-out sepia bodies glued into artificial arrangements. Elva, Ivo, Loba, and Earl perched on a limb stretched over the Arkansas River bluff and dangling from the limb tip. A final figure had her face cut-out: a dark head-less dress with raised arm, Elna, our absent mother.

We dropped the shovels in the shallow of the creek, al-ready blooded dark with red rock and fallen leaves. Gayla moved behind Elva and Ivo, leaned in to look at the pho-tograph book they had thought to bring, when they had forgotten food, our clothes, papers which would serve to identify us. I wanted to go back, make sure that what was there was gone, burning, but this was what I wanted, and I couldn't tell them this. When Gayla had asked me over their cloth-wrapped bodies, Have I done this, somehow? I hadn't said anything at all.

Gayla put her hand on Ivo's, pointed her finger to the trestle leg where, in the summer, after work, Earl had searched with us for freshwater mussels. Boots tossed onto the creek slope, a dull mule skin mark burned out against the iron frame. His suitpants rolled up above bony knees as he stepped, tenderfooted, toward us in the water, our skirts tied around our waists, Elva, Ivo, on the shore complaining we were too old for muddy toes, too old to drag our great-uncles in after us. Where had Loba been that day, still dragging along the walk to our house, slow in the heat, observant, watchful of the trim of neighbor's lawns?

Hadn't they become fathers of the oldest variety, these two? Even Loba came down from the porch in sisal-soled slippers each spring to shake the tall branches of the mulberry tree so the dark berries would collect in the yard, so we could scoop them up in handfuls into stone bowls, our bare feet spotted bruise black with ripe mulberries.

And Earl, who painted and repainted the pine board rope swing we'd requested till it was the exact color of red we craved, that deep red of overripe peaches, that collected in the orchards down the road from our house, rotting, waiting for winter. Were they not fathers, these two? This was something we never asked of each other, so small, so soundless it seemed.

From the sharp penetrations left by the bullets of a rifle behind glass, we knew at once that someone must have been there that day as each of us moved into the room with the dishes, with silver, while Ivo straightened doily place mats and tucked napkins under pistol-handled knives, while Elva at the piano played nervously, waiting for the bread to brown, a ragtime piece that mimicked a train collision, and as Gayla carried the étouffé pot and stopped to take the *stomp, stomp* that the sheet music called for in the pauses between measures, the stewpot sloshing in counterpoint waves.

Then each uncle idling in, stocking-footed. Loba from his pine rocker, Earl from the bench he'd made himself from the half-broken porchstep boards the year Gayla put her leg through trying to stomp a cricket. They sat, folded up papers, unfolded napkins, waited.

After they had fallen, the aunts huddled at their table end did not move toward their husbands but looked at you, first already slipping down under the tablecloth in a polite, silent faint. I was the one who thought to bury them. And why not, I had faced the window. I thought I had seen something there.

Now as we had gotten as far as the bridge and under the trestle Gayla gripped the shoulders of each aunt. She was confused somehow, so she could not place what had happened, and she had to ask the aunts if there had been some shady dealings or was this somehow her fault?

She did not mean to accuse them but they were accused. For where was our mother? The thin frame of her, elongated, stretched, as only we had seen it, dangling in mid-air? Surely not dead, as we had been told.

Gayla moved away from the aunts, let her question hang, I doubt she ever expected an answer. She waded into the November cold of the creek water to the mussel trestle where we had played at searching, collecting, our favorite games. And nearly submerged she squatted in the water, pulling her hands along the muddy bottom.

How could it have been her fault? Weren't we both inside the dining room, laying out silver, setting out the étouffé?

But I had seen something there. Something I could have stopped? Or something more diaphanous and a long time coming. A dark headless dress, moving in the poisoned berries of the pyracantha, stomp-stomping in time with my sister, a raised knee, a revealed stockinged ankle, a sharp-boned knuckle tapping silently on the glass in ragtime rhythm?

Her missing eyes watched us move, lined a sight, called us home.

—∿—

The Scent of Apples

I call your attention to the olive lapels of a hilltop dandy, Fennis, who stretches out his waterbird legs in the April grass of a ravine slope, the narrow back tires of his Hercules bicycle jammed, akimbo, between two rocks. The chain is broken. His cast-off raccoon coat has been carelessly lumped nearby in the grass and rests like a sleeping bear. His priggish ankles are sunlit and watery below pistachio hosiery. He rests, as he is easily taxed. Dashing! Look: a lavender sprig nosegay tucked in the mint-silk edge of his buttonhole.

An immense pinkish canine lolls his dripping tongue beside the Hercules and eyes the motionless dandy who sniffs the attenuated perfume of apple blossom wafting from the western slope. His orchard.

Far below him a silvery creek runs thinly through the ravine bottom, flashes over moss and rocks, and works its way into a tin race and up to the slow grinding shelves of a waterwheel. Here is the primary spectacle of an artificial ruin of a Renaissance cider mill commissioned by Fennis. Its imported non-functioning apple presses have been sanded smooth as if by a history of nourishing friction, its thatched roof has been forced to an early rot, the west wall has been chemically scorched. A spiral stairwell leads to a mill tower and a wrought-iron platform. From here, the countryside is shown to advantage. A lovely view from a lovely ruin.

Affixed to the pebbled drive of the artificial ruin is a genuine ruin. In this case, a trestle bridge, halfway collapsed, with dangling remnants. The remaining portion of bridge hangs like a pier over the ravine. In its incompletion, the half-bridge leaves Fennis separated from his only neighbors: a decrepit gourd farmer and his orphan ward, Mimsy. This separation only increases the curiosity of Mimsy who, as a child, peeks at Fennis through her thin, cupped fingers, and who, as a growing teen, even on tiptoes, can see only portions of his cider ruin and nothing of his home across the deep canyon, which lays at the top of a slender brick road. And Fennis's home is worth seeing: an ostentatious Japanese-style edifice, in which, on winter days, Fennis, a passionate recluse, sequesters himself and wanders about, got up in a green silk kimono and gaiters. He stumbles through half-open paper screens, glancing at a variety of obscure reference books, thinking highbrow and inconsequential thoughts. He pours tea from a pumpkin-shaped teapot, bulbous and globed, with a stem-topped stopper. He is alone with only the sounds of himself and his dog, whose enormous velvety paws pad across tatami mats and Persian rugs. There are brocaded, fan-backed armchairs, overstuffed chesterfield sofas, hand-carved banquettes, four poster beds with panel moldings, tambour roll-top desks, leather upholstered fainting couches, and other furnitures of an entirely non-eastern style which pack the house to its paper walls. In the largest screened studio, Fennis has rigged up an old-fashioned tripod-and-bellows folding camera to catalog his reclusive decline in self-portraits for city bohemians who follow his eccentricities from afar with disgust and envy.

The gourd farmer's ward is less estranged. Now a young lady, on damp summer evenings Mimsy slips down the ravine side and follows the creek to Fennis's decorative cider press ruin. She sniffs at the presses and climbs up to the mill tower. From here she can see into Fennis's home from her spyglass. She watches him creep about in Nile green crêpe de Chine robes. He spoons hollandaise from a pewter porringer and scans the spring catalogs, circling items with a charcoal marking pen. She sits through the night, well until the morning. At dawn, each day, Fennis emerges more worn and pale than the day before. He eats breakfast on the western rooftop deck, but as the toe of his gaiter steps into the morning light, Mimsy scrambles up the ravine, back to her guardian, afraid of being locked out.

Fennis, whose cordoned paper walls are lined with self-portraits, is a man who imagines he is in danger of being watched. He trusts the ominous aura of his half-bridge to protect his privacy from the neighboring hillside. He goes about his life without considering the gaze of a rapidly growing ward; rather, each year, he grows far more distracted and submerges himself in botanical studies. His passion is apples. Their cultivation, their passage into the world in sharp, crisp greens, and the tenuous snap of their flesh wrenched from dripping cores.

On one particular April morning, he stretches out in an Adirondack lounger, wrapped in rugs and mufflers, turbaned in wool, mirrored in the dark pool of his breakfast cup. He catches the whiff of apple-sweet air for the first time in many months. He casts off a pile of grassy chenille, suits himself in outdoor garb and full furs, and dashes out onto the frontmost porch of the japonica to the, until recently, snowbound Hercules, and pedals, huffing along the western winding path, until a small accident leaves his Hercules wedged in the mud.

Spilt on the grass as he is now, he catches a shallow breath and slows himself down. In the air is the scent of apple-blossom perfume. He is nothing if not rakish, a sprawled vision of spring.

In the small orchard, on the western slope of Fennis's hill, the pale early blossoms are peaking on the Mutsu Crispins. Fennis puffs into his orchard. His calves have atrophied from the long winter months, and his shoulders, humped over with mounds of raccoon, ache terribly. Yards ahead, the late fall Winesaps sit out the warmer climes; beyond them, the Cortlands have only just begun to leaf. The orchard is small but dense.

Fennis inspects his trees: leaves, blossoms, petals, pollination organs, trunks, bark, root knees. Most are well, with one exception: the base of the ninth Mutsu is scarred, gnawed and gashed as if by a giant bear. A bear in the Mutsus! Already the leaves of the lowest branches are speckled and translucent, their ruffled points curled in and slightly blackened. He puts a gloved finger in the flaking claw rut, and picks at the grain.

In a moment he has doffed his coat, his olive jacket, an embroidered waistcoat, a sparkling tourmaline watch fob, a long portion of muffler. He has hiked a significant cuff into his linen trousers and is showing a good segment of pasty shin below his sock garters; he has tucked in the olive tassels on his wingtip brogues and unloosed a foulard necktie. In another minute he is prying loose the orchard shed's door and foraging, then hauling, roughly, a laden wheelbarrow across the orchard. He tosses up, digs in, and pounds down a solid fencing of chicken wire and short posts around the ninth Mutsu. He casts an eye around, at the dozens of unprotected darlings, at the feeble wire and posts. His best labor is no match for a savage beast. He curses and stamps the mulch.

Even without his cast-off furs, the walk back to the wreck of the Hercules is a great deal for the waifish dandy who has dined this winter on sauces and teas. The dragging of the defunct bicycle has nearly done him in by the time he hauls it up on the frontmost porch of the japonica, and lays it to rest in its snowy crevice. Inside the house, he pulls himself through several paper screens to a room lined with books where a patinaed steamer trunk is draped with a verdigris tapestry: a Turkish swimming cat aswirl in sea foam. He pulls off the tapestry and pries open the trunk's lock. In the search he discards a hatching doll, a set of wind chimes, an unfortunate batik, a stale box of chocolates, a basket of erotic novelty soaps, until with clumps and clangs he hauls out a battered black telephone and a length of clear, flat cord.

In the foyer he shoves aside an elephant foot umbrella stand to reveal a dusty phone jack, where he plugs in the relic. Dials. Nestles into the earpiece.

Today as the sun rises, the dandy lolls again in his Adirondack lounge, wheezing softly below lap rugs. He sips a vegetable broth. On the southern slope, on a hidden back road, a stream of puffing tailpipes edges up the mountain toward the western orchard. There they begin an orchard wall of unusual density and height. The small park is awash with mechanics: flatbeds and graders, mortar-mixing machines on dolly wheels, a dump truck, five trucks of paving and cobble stones in twelve tones of grey, and a six-by-six packed full of stupored masons of varying age and size, in coveralls and clodhoppers, their fingers already locked on trowels. As the sun creeps, they scrape and level the sloped meadow on the orchard's edge. They lay out string runners around the parameter. They churn tanks of mortar; they set foundations, lay stones, dig in, line up, mark with chalk, and check the plumb.

It takes several days for the wall to finally begin to take shape, ankle high, then knee, another week, hip and shoulder, and so on until the masons hang limply from tall yellow scaffolding, and balance their whiskey-soaked limbs on two-by-fours.

Each day, from the ruin tower, Mimsy watches the orchard at dusk. So much activity is hardly imaginable.

The last breath of winter keeps Fennis from witnessing the progress of his orchard fortress. Elderly at forty-five, reclusive decline has left him hollow-chested and pinchy. He is struck with an ague unlike any he recalls from youth. He recedes indoors, not even risking the dawn breezes to examine his continental tabloids in natural light. Instead he huddles in robes and furs beside an open wing of a western-facing window and sniffs the deepening musk of the apple blossoms. He is beside himself to get to his orchard. Still the cool air lingers. He waits for a full-bosomed sun to warm the deck chairs and fill his dusty and echoing lungs.

Three April nights Mimsy crawls into the tower and peeks into the windows of the japonica. She sees what she has always known to be a nervously ambulatory dandy reclined on a sofa, his teeth chattering. Or she sees him ghostly pale, and dozing beneath a dozen hand-dyed peacock bed sheets. Three dawns pass without his movement toward the western deck for teas and sauces. On the fourth morning, she catches the flashing shine of a black car in the pebbled lot. The attending physician alights with a tray of elixirs in spectral array.

Another week passes, and Mimsy gives up the pretense of returning at dawn for breakfast with her guardian. Instead, she watches the rise and fall of the fitful snoozing chest of the bed-sick dandy, his lazing pooch drifting in and out between paper screens with his head tipped in confusion. Fennis, now, is so weakened he only gets up to warm a cream gravy, or sits all day in bed and dashes off watercolor sketches on long sheaves of rice paper, tossing them, meekly, to the floor.

The farmer's ward returns to the long barren gourd farm where her senile guardian wanders the vegetable garden in pajamas shouting commands at an absent crew of workers. He has long since forgotten he has a ward, thinks instead of the gourd blight of '07 and the subsequent moonlit field fires of that year. He circles the cantaloupe patch with a palm pressed to his brow. In the garden, Mimsy picks the succulent leaves of purslane to prepare a nourishing soup.

In the farm kitchen, the kettles are full blaze as she prepares an enormous supper for the waning dandy. Purslane soup, potatoes and pickled nasturtium buds, sliced avocado with lemon, a Persian herb pie of butterhead lettuce and fresh coriander stems, and a giant cucumber misery salad.

Today, the sun has receded and the sky has opened up in an April torrent that fills the ravine's creek. She is undaunted. The crossing is rough, but she manages. She carries the feast down into the ravine in a lavender-lined wicker basket, across the swelling creek, through the cider ruin, and up the brick path to Fennis's porch. There, with the front screen half opened to permit the free travel of the pinkish hound, the ward wanders into the house and silently sets out the dinner, on the floor, on a long jade tablecloth, below the poking nose of the house mutt.

She stops only for a second to take in an interior she has watched so often from her pirate's spyglass. By the door panel is a photographic self-portrait of Fennis in full dandy's garb as he poses with an oversized banana plant. She stashes the framed photo in her basket and heads for the door. She tugs the beaded bell pull with great force before she darts through the rain.

When she reaches the farm, she finds the doors locked. Her guardian cannot even recognize her, he is so lost in another decade. He assumes her some enemy of the gourd. He threatens her with a wrinkled and spotted fist from behind the leaded panes.

However, in the Japanese house, Fennis alights at the sound of the bell to find the carefully laid meal only partially nibbled by his pink mutt. He peers down the drive, past the ravine, but can see little from his porch and certainly not a now homeless orphan dripping in her lavender silks. The rich smell of fine food implores him. He begins the purslane soup, tears through the nasturtium potatoes, sucks down the avocados.

He finishes the meal with the misery salad, and the tartness of the dressing, and the bitterness of the greens, all is felt doubly by Fennis who is not used to sharp flavors. The garden shallots are so hot in this salad that they sting his nostrils and burn his eyes. Before long he is soaking in a stream of salad tears, which mar his nightgown in milky splotches.

Fennis ends the enormous salad with a sluice of tears pouring on the foyer's tatami mats. He feels exhaustion and hauls himself back to his bed.

The misery salad has a cleansing effect on the dandy. For the first time in weeks he sleeps a sound sleep and his dreams are not plagued by visions of fire blight, red-banded leaf hoppers, or fanged vermin. He sleeps for days.

When he awakens, his chest feels something more like a chest should, and he ambles out onto the western deck. Such time has passed! He sniffs the sticky scent of the already mulching petals of apple blossom. Their tiny green bulbs must be peeking.

Still in his mind is the nourishing repast, and he feels he knows the culprit. He drags himself into a suit of olive linen and moves slowly down the bricked drive to the cider ruin. With deliberate steps, he climbs the spiral stairs to the top of the mill. Across the ravine is the farmhouse, and inside, so he would guess, the salad maker. However, he sees only the slovenly wreck of a decrepit man in tattered pajamas, a burnished gourd helmet perched on his head. Where is the salad maker? He gives up his search and slinks down the wrought iron stairwell and back up the path, homeward.

Within the week, the elixir physician returns and examines Fennis. He finds him in suitable condition to return to the orchard but warns him that to tax himself again would be sure death. Fennis, in a fit of botanical joy, spends the evening at work on the spoke of the Hercules, replacing its shattered chain. In his bedroom, with full open windows, he lays out his garb and buffs his brogues to a high shine. He chooses a jacquard waistcoat with a holly print on ivory silk and hooks in the silvery watch and tourmaline fob.

Look at Fennis in his olive linen, rouge on his cheek-bones, a fresh lavender sprig boutonniere, once again his rakish self. He jounces on the mended Hercules with his hound close behind. He takes it slow down the curving western path, through the meadow, to his freshly mortared orchard citadel. He is determined not to tax himself.

The masons however have been careless. The heavy iron gates have been left ajar. Muddy tracks lead into the orchard where Fennis creeps on new-buck soles, leery of the sharp claws which mauled the ninth Mutsu.

The Mutsu retains her boundary fence however, and the scene is just as he left it, though in the wheelbarrow, a furry mound is huddled, its back rising and falling, its breathing labored and shallow. He approaches it, pokes it with a discarded post, notes the raccoon pelt, and watches as it curls over. She shows a lavender silk breast, an absinth pallor, a leafy, tangled coiffure. Her chest-plate is a photograph of a rakish dandy with a potted banana plant.

There is something to her, some rotting sweet perfume, some mealy softness, and before he has even thought to check the tiny spring fruits, their leaves, their hardening branches, he is dragging her barrow out the gate, eastward with a stumbling tread, huffing toward the Japanese house, even as the ague empties him again, and his body whistles like a cut flute. He stumbles and sniffs at her: throat, shoulders, muddy shoes. On her is the rotten scent of apple blossom. The smell and the flavor thicken in his mouth and throat.

—∞—

She Came from the East

I.

Within the island brig, where the framework is troubled by rats, escape is through a gnawed wall. In the space behind the plaster a crosshatching of pathways forms an intricate lace.

First, so many nights with little sleep, or when he slept he imagined his narrow mattress surrounded, a twitching crowd just out of reach of the sweep of his hands. Daily, he paced the cell and counted the steps or knocked on the wall. No response beyond their scuttle. Then a cleft in the enclosure and a parting of the tissue; he looked through the wall as though through a window. All this before the dark eyes of an anxious gathering. Finally, a fevered swim through counterfeit storms, or mechanical waves. Afterwards, the pallor of sodden ash for the returning lad.

He appeared on the dock as if by request, his jacket damp in the spray, his shoulder weighed down with ropes, his kit and topcoat toggled, and in bracelets.

It was always time to move elsewhere. She had freshly arrived from the east. Her hair was well-gilded, and her dress crisply layered like a pastry. The stateroom was paneled in marbled maple, and the bed situated on a pedestal of drawers and shelves, a cramped nest, or a crawlspace. She examined her face in the glass. A vine divided the mirror. The rupture offset her peculiar eyes. This was nothing new. Madam appeared always in two disguises. Sweetbriar with soft petals and hooked thorns. Made up gold, and with elixir voice, she soon alighted on the gangplank with clear intention. Nor had she traveled on the boat from which she seemed to emerge.

A mariner's low dive abutted the pier. From the open door a flag of light cut across the dock boards. A rascal behind the counter slung beer and gin. A dock-side crimp positioned himself at the bar's corner, attempting to shanghai a cabin boy in tall socks and short trousers. A slatternly blonde attended the trio in peaked caps gathered around a whiskey drum. They yarned in oaths and blasphemes.

She followed him through the low jamb; the atmosphere disrupted upon entry. Her heels rang on the floorboards. She was outlined in white. The men showed an unwelcome curiosity. She took her whiskey neat. She had no local knowledge, but it was good to always be returning home.

For a time, he sunk into the drink. Later, outside the dive, they collided in loose tackle.

I'm between ports, she told him.

What a coincidence.

I've had my eye on you all evening.

You've had *your* eye on *me*?

You come highly recommended.

Sure, I do. But for what?

I need a pilot for the rough stuff. I plan to yacht in the Baltic.

How did you figure you'd get there from here: by way of the Panama Canal?

I like to take things as they come.

So do I, but they so rarely do.

———

On the yacht, the saloon was plush with lounges and cushions. It was a private affair with pheasant under glass. The harbor was still, but the pier seemed to shift. A thin sallow steward, in fringed epaulet and gold-laced cap, appeared with the salad. She offered him a brandy, and her wristlet chimed on the crystal. He shot her a cagey, ruttish look. She returned it with a dipped chin. Through a topside skylight, a mothering type gave him a quick glowering once-over. A young brunette in a black silk nightdress was disembarking leeward, followed by a slim man in evening clothes and no shoes.

You have someone for everything on this boat, the sailor said. I can't imagine what you want with me.

It's not such a large craft as that.

No? Who was that then? He inclined his uncombed head.

Which?

The dark-haired girl dressed up like an upstairs maid where there's no upstairs.

Just a friend.

And her friend?

A cousin of mine.

He forgot to lace up his tap shoes?

Yes, well. He's particular about the damp.

That's why I try to stay away from boats.

———

They could sit on any wall; every thing was a bench and above it a vista through glass. After such a dark bottle an obligation took root. Chinese New Year's fireworks overhead. A mingling of eyes. Several moments began and were interrupted. The air was invested. Another long while spent on the boat but in close proximity to the shore. However, in the saloon, a seat remained empty.

As the thick perfume of the linden draws a bee, the question becomes *who* is collecting? Accumulate, then dissimulate behind the disguise. As a matter, finally, the professor slipped up on wheels. One fold of a lap robe tore in the catches of the motorized chair. His knees propped against each other in a narrow tent. His toes threatened to slip from their perch.

For a husband, he didn't yield much. His sensation was disintegrating. He was made of as little charm as the space he took up. The sum total was only a pile of scraps from a motionless existence: bloodless lips and a face of sloughed bark. Lead-cast eyes under dry white lashes. Ears dissolved into his head. A suited, slouched bird, he sat in a cone of shadow.

II.

So begins the first night of many recorded in the log. The chart of evening: a nautical chart. It is written in the language of passenger vessels, yachts for crossing or cruising. Wherein the eye makes a mystery of the clues. His position was above board. Hers mostly below. So he followed her every movement on the boat.

Obviously, the misleading part is to be brought in on something, to be hired into the family, so the sailor noted, though the specifics of his detail had yet to be presented. With one in the barrel, why had she collared him? What did she expect him to carry, or crack? Still there was no reason not to be hopeful. It might all come down to a quiet moment of friendly persuasion.

They made their way along the coast. A boat with full service and an ever-shifting crew. He tended the helm. She lounged about in belted trunks and spoke to each of them in a different language.

Follow the chart, the one which shows the narrow peel of shore, adjacent to the islands, between each and every one a channel or sands. The flood was rising. Aground in sand, against which the boat stutters. Now go to sleep so as to awaken for a few hours.

―――――――

They talked between meals, between swims, between sleeping. Nights, he preferred to keep the wheel.

The role of wife has certain challenges, she confided. With a genius, even more so. Tell me a war story.

I don't like to be graphic in front of mixed company or mixed drinks.

That's a good policy. I wish I could follow it. I'd like to be sure of things. I have something in mind.

You've got a large staff already.

I will need more pronounced physique for the job I have in mind.

He began a long story that involved a small boat, a large boat, the enemy, and a blonde to whom he'd never said "I love you." There was much more to it: he'd stabbed a piano player on one of the islands, and blown taps for a friend on the naval base—when had he learned his General was actually his father?—AWOL and incognito, he had lost himself in a raft and drifted for days, washed aground again, and the spray of the beach had come up over his shoulders as he lay half-conscious against a rock, wild with a fever, when the enemy had come aground to search for turtles for soup. He'd been lost out there a long time. He'd imagined a nurse or a nun had joined him. He'd imagined quite a few things, but for the report he kept it brief. He limited it to the large boat, the small boat, and a fire on the bridge, and tapped his leg which rasped dully of oak below the knee.

I never knew, she told him.

Now, it's your turn.

I have a great war story, she said. The guy was married. And he had another girlfriend already. He loved to get us all together, like friends, so he invented some vacations. Weird vacations, sort of mythic treks, and I only went on one: to a cabin in the Black Forest.

We traveled down in cars, all the ladies together. We stopped off for a bite, and before I knew it, I'd been stranded in the little village. I found them in a teashop. How they all loathed me. And the man was nowhere to be seen.

When he showed up, he barely noticed me. I thought I was vying for his attentions. It's a joke really. I don't even try that hard, usually. But here's the amazing part. The cabin's kitchen floor gave off to a water hole of some kind, like an underground spring. And then—I don't know where it came from—a red rose just hit the top of the water. I dove in immediately. The entire adventure had been about the search for mermaids. I saw one under the water, but she had legs. She was beautiful, and I could recognize this while the other girls couldn't and were wont to have jealous fits.

What else did I find there? A pile of gold doubloons. I pulled them up from the sand. Gold doubloons, ha! They were obviously coins from a much later date, and they were marked with faces of matinee idols. But I had no idea. (He's not interested in money, you see. Even though he *should* be interested in money.) In fact, and I was saying to myself at the time, He is going to love this stuff, but I should have known better. Do you see what I'm saying: This does not show that I understood the guy, but that I always think I'll get lucky. Do you believe me?

Of course.

About the mermaids?

Why not? What happened to the guy?

I don't know. Back to his harem I guess. It doesn't matter. I was due back on the boat.

Why tell me all of this?

It was recent.

At your age, it's all recent.

It was a short row from the yacht to the vacationer's island. Now beginning the off-season, the beaches had a desperate look, and the waters were more unpredictable. At the sea-facing hotel someone was going from window to window drawing in the striped awnings. Only a few stalwarts wandered on the boardwalk.

A fateful day for swimming, perhaps. From a narrow cliff, she dove. After a time she surfaced limply, a false show of being knocked out. He cosseted and fondled the remains. She made signs of reviving before sinking further into the sand.

There's something more between us. Something you don't want to say, he suggested.

I learned that feeling in another language. It won't translate.

The way a song never comes across if you're not singing it?

It's like this: going through a maze, you can make so many turns. You may get to the center, but it could take awhile. At some point along the way, maybe you forget the center. You can love in so many directions, you know.

What a lot of hooey.

Maybe it is, but it is what I was taught. And there is more to it. However you go into the maze, you've got to come out of it the same. That's all I know about that feeling.

We're talking about two different things. You've got me all wrong.

No, I haven't. I've got you exactly at your word.

The beach grasses kept sentry. In view of the boat, they lodged in the rut of beach. The husband, on deck, admired them on their spacious shore. Like a hunter and a sprite, until examined through a series of magnified lenses.

Well beyond the beach, a giant Ferris wheel turned, unlit, awaiting dusk. Also, the faint sound of a hurdy gurdy.

———

On that same day, the inventors arrived on the yacht. There were numbers of them in white coats and dark glasses. They carried their clipboards and their pockets bulged. They gathered around the professor, taking down information and measuring, like so many tailors. The most eloquent among them approached in soft soles.

You'll want to anchor for the duration, the inventor told the sailor. We'll be coming and going as we please for a few days.

After their first departure, they left several cages of their test subjects. In the days which followed, the chatter of the boat began to collect, and the sailor recognized, finally, a familiar group of friends.

———

All the servants were discharged, only the pilot remained in employ. The professor removed himself to his stateroom, for days, with the boat anchored in the cove of the small island. Then, slowly, they began to overtake the large saloon. Through the saloon skylight he could see the form of the professor stretched out on a lounge, bundled to the throat in rugs. He stared blankly into the harangue of the creators.

Meanwhile, she moved about the boat in white lab coat, surrounded by the inventors. She adopted all the jobs of the crew: the galley, the service, the sustaining tasks of ropes and rigging. They were stilled, and there was little for him to do. He observed the cages of the test subjects, which dwindled and replenished in the passing days. They sucked on tubes and turned in wheels. They seemed to say something he could almost make out. Evenings, he rowed into the island, where he prowled the boardwalk and the amusements.

———

On one such night, he found her waiting in his quarters. She had cast off her lab jacket and was slinking behind her hair. She popped up briefly to give him a summary look of the coming speech. Her eyelids showed red. It was hard to say if it was exhaustion or exposure.

I think it's time for you to go, she told him. What I want, you can't give me.

What about these scientists? he asked. What can they do?

They can do anything. What they can't create from scratch, they can modify. They can mechanize. I should be proof enough of that. You don't think I'm like I am by nature?

It doesn't matter much. We're both stuck here.

I have a passion for disappearing.

I know all your haunts.

You just don't get it, she said. Whether I want it or not, whether I deny it or not, two animals may trace a common path, but every time the trail of it gets demolished by the next animal. Everything, every trace just gets scattered. You can't go on thinking you're the only one. You just can't. It doesn't jibe.

I have a few canned adages too, you know. No one ship-wrecks himself and goes willing up in smoke.

You don't know women. Or men for that matter.

And what have you learned about men, with the company you keep?

Senseless things. Their incurable moods. Their thirst for uproar. Their arbitrary discretions. It's enough to show you that it's better not to hang around any relations, once the action is over.

It's a hard way of thinking, he told her.

He had an effect on her she hadn't anticipated. As always, when she saw someone so large, with this churlish torso, she imagined him dancing lightly in suede shoes and hunting tweeds, under rising mists. The sailor was even harder to reconcile. He refused to flit. Though he would have to. Hers was necessarily a vision of the expendable.

———

The weather was turning. August storms had already begun. Even the sheltered cove began to rock. The boat pitched and took on water. He readied the dink. Then he burst in on them, unannounced.

In the saloon, she spooned him his supper. He seemed to be keeping up a light, quiet dialog, in spite of the pitching. With the lap rugs cast off, the sailor got the first idea of the boat's progress. The professor's hands had been replaced with the paws of a lion. On the arms of his chair, his furred knuckles were pulsing.

We've got to get off the boat.

He won't be moved, she said.

Can't you see he's done for.

You're wrong about that, the professor told him. I'm gaining strength by the minute. Soon my doctors will be here with me. And your time is about up.

From within her nursing apron, she removed the pearl-handled pistol. A low bearing shot. It lodged in the silk of the sofa. A scuffle, and a series of strikes. The weapon, inevitably, changed hands. Still, she made her way topside and overboard. He piled roughly into the rowboat, and cast himself off. Slow going, but he had her in sight. She outstripped him still, and made her way on shore. Over his shoulder, a raucous laughter poured forth from the lit saloon.

The park, after dark, had no pedestrians. The funhouse maze was an open mouth. Only partly fanged. Each turn was veiled with a beaded curtain which cast shadows in strands at crossbars. Several woven intersections. A string of pearls on her neck, she led the way. The sailor followed. The husband tottered behind, a boxing doll, loaded with shot. He supported himself on paws, on canes.

The pistol report. In the broken mirror, she split at the waist and, top heavy, her torso threatened to slip off. Again, he looked through a shattered window. As with lines over the lens of a camera, the fracture followed the object. He moved across the broken glass.

She was not very vacuous, though she was still working out the minor points, a story which began in windows and ended in mirrors, and nothing cleanly cut.

———

Eyes like a name, her eyelids flicker. The iris capsizes. A murderer is rarely moved. Behind him, the trail of his reflection in shards. The pursuing inventors. Forward, the ruined beach.

—⧑—

Entertainment

An ingénue distinguished herself briefly on film by skipping rope in the background of a single musical number, a vaudeville stage act. The act was a peach: in front of a park bench, two rival lovers in pin-stripped jackets and straw boaters sought the affection of a cover-girl by displaying their singular talents: the hoofer tapped in circles around a crooner, whose dipping vocals left the audience in swoons. The stage act was only a sideline; the dancer was a gambler and the singer a hotel concierge, and both were anxious to get back to their livings and leave the stage behind. The hoofer took a boat headed for Monte Carlo, and the crooner hopped a train for the Catskills. Both ended up in Rio, where the cover-girl had turned revolutionary and tucked her lovely red hair up in a scarf. She convinced the boys to pitch in on a kidnapping. The crooner took a job as the concierge of a hotel where a renowned Russian ballerina was staying. The hoofer milled about playing cards, and watched the ballerina with malicious intent. The crooner lent all his concentration to love: his revolutionary cover-girl. By the time the ballerina finally fell for the attentions of what she thought was a shifty gambler, he'd fallen for her too. The gig was already up for the crooner—whose drunken serenade from the previous night had not gone over—when he stood below the ballerina's window by mistake. The cover-girl misunderstood the hoofer's story of "a friend" in love with a famous ballerina. She'd broken with politics, and all her hopes hung on the crooner. She took off for home in sunny California. The crooner followed. The hoofer held the bag: his ballerina inside and no point of delivery. The kidnapping she could get over, but she'd had it with dancers years before. She took off for sunny California. The hoofer followed. The cover-girl swore off politics. The crooner gave up hotels. The hoofer had never had much of a poker face. Only on the stage could all this get sorted out. Needless to say the film was a terrific hit.

The rope-skipping ingénue got her notice too. She was cast in her own lead part: singing and dancing in a big budget production. As it turned out she couldn't dance, though this is no great surprise. It doesn't necessarily follow that rope-skipping is the same as dancing, and she was in over her head with a newer, fresher dancing heart-throb. And could he dance! He wore his trousers with a special cuff to show off his feet. He was not so pleased with her, and let her know. It was somewhat later that she found herself huddled under a piano on a soundstage, in tears. The stage was almost entirely dark, so that when someone came in to rehearse, she almost didn't recognize the gambling hoofer from her first film. He was so intent on learning a new piece of choreography, he didn't see her crouching below the piano. He was much older now, of course. He began slowly and stiffly and nothing looked quite right. His face grew so pained and unpleasant, and for the several hours that passed, he continued only in the near dark of the half-dressed stage.

—⁓—

In Guffy's Plum Cricket

The trouble with Marty began on a Thursday, at Guffy's Plum Cricket, where there is a bar *and* a grill. We are snaking our way into a circular booth, when the waiter asks for drinks. I say Cherry Coke, the waiter says, Roy Rogers? Right. It's like that every time, Cherry Coke, I say, Cherry Coke, Marty says. Two Roy Rogers? The waiter is a rank, hippie type, someone who's been using one of those deodorant rocks rather than a legitimate roll-on so that when he passes by the booth his stench wafts over us. He is back from the bar with two plastic tankards, darkly scarlet, an inordinate number of maraschinos floating on the meniscus. Two Roy Rogers, he says when he puts down the glasses. He takes our grill order. It's late afternoon, the front door propped open to the dusty outside light, and the Cricket is winding up from mostly-grill to mostly-bar. We focus on the TV over the booth, which is muted but captioned, where a war film is playing in dull hues. I say, *Guns of Navarone*! and Marty says, great. Have you seen it? I say. Isn't that the one with Gregory

Peck? he says like he's seen it, like somehow knowing that it's the one with Gregory Peck means he's seen it, and in saying, isn't that the one, etc., I will respond, yeah that's the one, and go on talking while he sits there pretending to have seen it, never having seen it. So I say, Marty, don't say 'Isn't that the one with Gregory Peck' as a means of pretending to have seen it if you haven't seen it. Have you seen it? And he says no. No, he says, no I haven't seen it.

I am livid, but I sit quietly and slurp my Roy Rogers, passively hating Marty. I can't decide what I hate most about Marty at this moment: whether it is that he intended on sitting there pretending to have seen *Guns of Navarone*, never having seen *Guns of Navarone*, maybe even making an off-the-cuff remark about it, for instance, saying of Gregory Peck, I liked him better in *Spellbound*, or that he deliberately hasn't seen *Guns of Navarone* in the first place. I am saying in my mind, How is it that I've ended up out here at Guffy's Plum Cricket with someone who hasn't seen *Guns of Navarone*? And it's like when I found out Marty's middle name was Robin and I said, Marty Robbins? And he said, hmm? and I said, Down in the West Texas Town of El Paso? And He said hmm? again and I felt a pang of something like passive hatred.

Marty watches the screen and waits to see if I will go on and say whatever it is I am wanting to say about *Guns of Navarone* until he can't stand just sitting there with me fully aware that this is maybe the first time he's ever heard of *Guns of Navarone*, and finally he says, That David Niven is mighty effeminate, which is off-the-cuff, of course, and even worse than if he'd said, I liked him, meaning Peck, better in *Spellbound*, since in this case he is basing his judgment on captions, or moreover, as I suspect, basing it on some preconceived contemptuous notion of David Niven, which is, frankly, personally-motivated. Whereas if he'd said, I liked him better in *Spellbound*, meaning Peck, it would have only *intimated* contempt for *Guns of Navarone*.

I know that I have to say something when the grill food arrives, so I say, I liked him [meaning Peck] better in *Spellbound*, to which Marty says, Oh have you seen *Spellbound*? as though he's holding the monopoly on *Spellbound*, a question he has asked me every time either Peck or Hitchcock has come up in the past two years to which I usually say, Yes, yes I've seen *Spellbound*, don't ever ask me again if I've seen *Spellbound*.

But I don't say it this time, instead I begin to actively hate him. I say, I'm actively hating you, he says, What's new? and pretends to continue watching *Guns of Navarone*, not as though he is genuinely interested in *Guns of Navarone*, but as though he is deeming to watch *Guns of Navarone* due to its unstated importance to me, as though watching *Guns of Navarone* is a self-sacrifice, a sacrifice he is willing to make since I am unreasonably unstable, and since, in his mind, I have never seen *Spellbound*. It is as though there are two poles: *Spellbound* pole, which marks well-reasonedness, even-keeledness, understated good taste, and *Guns of Navarone* pole, which marks hysteria and backwardness.

In his mind, he is *Spellbound* while I am mired in *Guns of Navarone.* Moreover, even the suggestion that I have seen *Spellbound,* that I might be somehow part of *Spellbound,* is impossible for him to get his mind around. He continues to sit, convinced I've never seen *Spellbound,* that I've never had the good sense to have seen *Spellbound,* that I've gotten this far with only *Guns of Navarone.* Yes, I say, yes, I've seen *Spellbound.* What was it you liked better about him [Peck] in *Spellbound?* he says as a way of testing me. And it occurs to me that maybe I have only recently seen *Spellbound* after many months of claiming to have seen *Spellbound,* and that anything, at any moment could give me away, so first I say, His hair was better in *Spellbound,* and then I remember and I say, the surreal dream is better, and it occurs to me that I must have seen it as a child, that I've been carrying around the sense of that movie as a surrealist dream for years, that it has been nothing more to me than Gregory Peck slipping down an abstracted mountain slope, though I'm not convinced it was Peck at all. I say, the surreal dream is better. Though as I think of it more, the tumbling, the mountain, Gregory Peck, in my mind I'm sure it isn't tumbling at all but scaling, and the mountain isn't surreal, abstracted, but just darkened at midnight, and I must be thinking of the mountain climbing scene from *Guns of Navarone.* I've decided this surreal dream from *Spellbound* has nothing to do with *Spellbound,* but is entirely *Guns of Navarone,* so I say, No, I take it back, nothing is better in *Spellbound,* everything about Peck is better in *Guns of Navarone,* everything about it is better than *Spellbound*, and I am speaking the absolute truth.

But Marty isn't listening because he's watching the screen as Anthony Quinn strips the dress from the scarless back of the pale Greek traitor. He says, He's stripped her dress off, she's some sort of traitor. Look, he says, no scars! No scars equals traitor! He's right, there are no scars, even though each time I've watched this I've been half expecting them spreading out across her back like a topography. No scars, I say, and he thinks I'm coming around, I'm amiable again, we are finally coming to the same point. But we aren't and I can't help but hate him, stuck as I am in this impermeable space, hysteria, backwardness, and I know now I must be quiet if I want to move into *Spellbound,* a space where the bar is quite white and the floor below me is pitched and I am either scaling or slipping.

—⁓—

The Actor at Dinner

Ladies and Gentlemen, I give you the greatest actor of our time, we were told by our host. No one appeared. The name was unfamiliar. The door stood swinging, as the soup was brought in, cutting the view of the corridor forward and back, with no one in sight. Already, it was an awkward dinner party of no more than eleven. The conversation was not loud enough to cover so conspicuous an absence. Brace yourselves, we were told, he has the lightest touch ever.

On that belated cue the actor pushed into the dining room in plaid high-waisted trousers and a velvet waistcoat, the tips of his black moustache waxed, and curled up toward his eyes. His arms sent out a marvelous tremor that set the bouillabaisse rippling up over the tureen's lip. Every part of his body was violently attacking a role. Look at his throat veins, someone to my left shouted, they are coursing with anticipation and bloodlust. His shins, one of us said, his shin bones are the Laurence Olivier of shin bones. Bloody hell, another put forward, he has more expression in his corneas

80

than I've felt in my entire life. A pretty young girl with strong sensibility fainted under the effect, our host laughed, openly gloating. I was left speechless gazing at the wafting hint of mournfulness that slipped up the delicate curve of the actor's ankle below its scarlet stocking.

Suddenly, I was struck with the inevitability of the finale. How can this amazing creature sit down before us and eat his soup? But with a hand gesture of marked closure, he completed his arrival as abruptly as it had begun, and lifting his coat-tails, seated himself across from me, lips drawn, eyes downcast. The slightest blush of a smile appeared below his whiskers as he motioned to the host for a bolster to tuck against the small of his back in the dining chair. There was nothing remarkable to the manner in which he realigned the silver beside his plate. He picked up his soup spoon, sorted out a shiny mussel, and chewed in the customary manner. Before long, the purr of the conversing table rose to a thoughtless clamor. I, however, kept on with his breathtaking performance, as he dipped the corner of a napkin in his goblet to clean the broth from his waistcoat and brushed from his pant legs the crumbled traces of a French roll. Every gesture was studied precision. No part of him gave away the deadly exhaustion held up in his reedy chest, his absent utterance, the violent pulse below starched cuffs.

—◊◊—

Ghosts and Lovers
a novel in shorts

A story which begins in Budapest ends in Marseille.

Born in the teeth of a gale, the sailor was a gypsy drawn
from the sea. Later, on dry land at the turn of a century, my
father in short-pants followed the caravan of wagons covered
in moons and stars. He wore rings in his ears and a shirt
made of scarves. First, they roamed together. He grew en
route, though soon returned to the sea. Once, in Barcelona,
he slept in the streets. My mother was only a girl when they
first met, and already a bride. I arrived in a timely fashion,
then we moved on together. The accident which followed,
by his account, came as a great shock. She had fallen from
a train crossing the border. For many years, I had only this
image of her moving very quickly through the air toward the
slope along the tracks. He kept no photographs.

In the attic, I found a trunk. Their letters told of terrific passion. First, she read the fortunes of young girls in cards and
leaves. In her absence, I had developed a similar talent. My

own fortune was always murky: forwards and backwards in haze and clouds.

In my youth, I was given to visions swirling up in the steam of the soup pot. I feared poison in all foods, and I had grown suspicious. What had really become of her? Years later, I watched my father take the floor in a vicious tango and imagined the way in which I had come to belong to a man.

I entered my bloom and began my travels. I played the orphan and escaped to the circus, where high above the crowd I watched a pale Frenchman on the trapeze. His forehead curved upward, his hair outward in two bright points, and his shoulders formed a square, and his waist an S, and his legs, only two legs dangling, and his arms stronger with each passing day. We passed into courtship. I left no clues. If I was the tortured party, I kept up a scrim. I suspected his love was frivolous. My father's letters had taught me that with true passion comes threat and a struggle for breath. And so I went on in a gay affair. We had only a few phrases in a common tongue, though no matter. If humans were meant to speak in language, it is only to stand in for the words we have not yet formed in letters.

Our circus traveled by train, and in this way we put a great deal of distance between starts and stops. I tended the puppets, and wound the carillon, and folded the sandwich boards. At the back of my mind, I remembered my father and kept to the kitchen. Inside its sugar cage, the meringue cake nested. Leaves, at first tightly balled, unfurled in the cup. I strained the clumping custard and fell into a trance, awakened much later in the tent of the story-teller who began her tale as follows:

The future is fluid, but the past is final. A lovely Spanish gypsy was saved from suicide by a wealthy man who fell in love with her. Though she did not love the man, and so forth, when finally she capitulated, they served a tiered cake, the color of butter, but the marzipan groom cracked off at the legs. She met a Hungarian sailor who slept in the streets, and so began the affair, and she wept softly on the topmost floor, and her tears glinted in the light, and were noticed by strangers passing in the street. A great sorrow and a great beauty. Then the child was born. The sailor overwhelmed with jealousy poisoned her and stole her daughter. Both perished at sea. Alas, the gentleman went mad, and wept softly, tears glinted in the window of his office, in the garret of the villa. A great grace and a great sorrow. Now, I'll sing the song of this story in Catalan…

I stopped her at that. That last thing I wanted was the past revealed. The waves had taken us under twice, and we awoke on the shore. He tucked me in his coat. Still, when I felt fatherless, as often I did, I worked my way back to the water, my violent first lover.

Sorrowfully, the time had come to move on. Somewhere near Arles we had a beautiful off-evening. Then I left him treading the high-wire.

And so I traveled under an assumed name to Barcelona
where my mother had been born, and where she had been
poisoned. I found the home of a gentleman whose name I
had heard under the point of a circus tent. I ingratiated myself to a manservant named Javier. Each night, we stayed up
late playing Canasta.

Who does the cooking here? I asked.

Mostly me, he told me, but I'm no great hand. For years
I have been trying to convince my gentleman to hire a cook.
He prefers things bland and unskilled.

I know what he's missing, I said.

The next night Javier smuggled me into the kitchen and
I made a meal I had dreamed a hundred times: to begin,
Fetge d'Anec, a thick duck liver with caramelized quince, the
main course *Mongetes amb Calamarsets*, lovely baby squid
in white beans; there were vegetables roasted in hot ashes, a
giant pot of stewed chickpeas with chorizo and for dessert
crema catalana which jiggled under its sugar crust.

I watched as the gentleman seated himself at an exquisite
dressed table. His suit was contemporary, but in my eyes he
had an untimely swashbuckling quality held in a silver swish
of hair poised carefully over his forehead. When the meal
was finally served, he fainted. And what was it? I knew what
he was seeing: her small body twitching on the rug beneath
the table, convulsing modestly as blood slipped down the

side of her mouth onto the starched front of her dress. Javier splashed him in the face with a cool glass of tempranillo.

Where did you get this meal? he asked his manservant. But Javier remained speechless. This, he said, was the exact meal which poisoned my wife twenty years ago. I emerged from my place at the shadowed sideboard. Again, he fainted, and again was revived with the wine. Here a portrait came alive before him. The ghost, so long awaited, finally appears.

From there the memory fractures. I installed myself in a new father's house, and waited, and in those first weeks I kept my kitchen in afternoons and by evening. By mornings, I wandered confused in my mother's city, in reverie and in trance, as if taken with fever. Before me, a million futures unfolded, and even passing along the crowded streets my mind thickened with images, as so many planes on a cut gemstone: a woman and her lady's maid peeled apples into a great barrel while singing a noble harvest waltz in Russian. I walked in a great roundel of autumn leaves. Across a black glass stage, a giant dog, in waistcoat and foulard, approached me walking upright. I had yet to perfect any particular talent for arranging narrative along a clear line.

I stirred the eggs poaching in the cazuela. With a delicately curved knife, I shucked the mussels. I arranged the lobster on his bed of ice and lemons. My mother arose again from the steam of the stock pot, finally to speak:

> I climbed a ladder formed in sorrow, the details of which you have yet to discover.

In my garret, where below me my gentleman paced restlessly through the night, I practiced divination. I whetted and honed, and returned each day to the city, to regard the facets.

Once I read a fortune in tea leaves of an old woman, the landlady of a crumbling house for wayward types: those who travel incognito and slink through the streets of Barcelona darkly clad and ominous, in leather, wearing eye-patches and sweaty bandanas tightly tied at the throat. What could she do but take in degenerates to creep about her attic in the after hours? To slip through her kitchen in the gray before dawn in indigo pea coats, before fanning out thinly, to disappear on lesser highways and in unsavory ships.

She was so poor the water in her pipes ran nearly red from rust and her tea leaves were badly tainted. What could I tell her? Things were so murky. I could hardly admit I was a self-taught Hungarian. I looked closely. A knife fight? A decorative stiletto? A blood-curdling scream? It hardly seemed a fitting end to describe for someone so frail and delicate. I shrugged. She shook her head.

Nothing familiar? Are you looking carefully? she asked me with polite skepticism.

I am looking very carefully, but things are still muddled. A thin worm of intestine crept out from the gape at a man's side.

The leaves at the bottom of the cup were pale as pewter slivers. The powerful smell of mineral sediment rose out of the cup. What was there in this? The blue wool of a fisherman's sweater cut from chest-bone to navel drifting up on the beach?

Have you got a son at sea? I asked her.

She looked hopeful. I have a daughter in Perpignan who makes jewelry.

Have these leaves been steeped before?

Not per se, she told me.

Polluted?

An unsavory term.

Somewhat adulterated?

We sometimes must economize. There are my borders to think of.

She was right. In the leaves were swimming a dozen fates of the blackest water and her own scant future was overshadowed and washed-out.

I'm self-taught, I told her. I need more practice. I'll never sort this out. I'll come another day, and try with cards. She was unconvinced, but hardly saddened. In her mind, something glorious was unfolding, a silken vision of a grim future from within the pale leaves. The fantastic, the unthinkably thick swirl of a sudden change.

Once when I was purchasing salted herring in La Boqueria, I thought I heard a circus carillon and I remembered the trapeze artist I had once loved. By this time, I had come to understand that my gentleman had fallen in love with me because I resembled the wife who had been poisoned so long ago. There was something about my eyes, my hair, my nose, my gait, my laugh, my garlic äioli; it was never entirely specific. But that morning, in La Boqueria, it occurred to me that I might be in love again. How could I not be? The atmosphere was perfect, and even my room at the top of a ladder on the third floor of the gentleman's home seemed helplessly wedged over his sleepless scuttling. He had found my mother's letters among my things, just as I had found them among my father's. We were together in this. In the early hours of the morning, I tiptoed about in stockings, creaking the boards above him. He was terrified that I was the ghost of his dead wife, flittering about the house in skimpy nightgowns. I sprinkled dusting powder through the cracks of his ceiling and watched as his face paled under the shimmering mist. Here things stayed the same night after night, and each morning I could wake up and go to La Boqueria to choose the food for that night's dinner. And only if the wind was perfect would the sound of the circus carillon provide an impossible plague.

In time my gentleman and I fell in together. I recall the silent step of his kid boot on the ladder between floors. True, he was beautifully coiffured, and his nails smelled of milk soap, and his tail coat hung smartly against the backs of his knees (just as it had on the dog in my daydream). True, his light touch on my wrist kept me momentarily enflamed. The images of his future were always the same: this house, its roof in curved clay tiles, the whitewash flaking, and the garden of wild thyme. A man quite perfectly settled passes from youth to death in a single place. I was failing to see in him what my mother had failed to see, and what curled about thickly behind the eyes of those sailors littering the docks, whose bodies had become only two legs treading, in water as on land. By day, I ambled. I meandered. I flitted about. Then I returned to the same spot.

Was I short a father, or had I one to spare? I recalled those hands which so long ago had carved a little skiff for me from lye soap. In my tub, it bobbed along on the undulating surface, before, grown sleepy and unthinking, I snatched it up and scrubbed my arms and legs till the shape gave way to a thin crescent moon, as I sang: Oh, little caravan, oh little wagon, covered in stars, and beneath the stars, I'll trail at your wheels, my hound at my heels, little wagon, little wagon, all covered in stars.

Was I a ghost? Was I part devil? My lover watched me with his careful eyes. He perused my belongings. In the dark, on his cool patio, against the distant sound of the Mediterranean, he confronted me, gently with dignity, quickly rising to a hysterical tenor. Where had I gotten his dead wife's letters? Where indeed if a daughter had been lost at sea. I gave away the few facts I had to offer. And so I had to hear the tale a third time through, again, as it shifted and reshaped. My father put poison in a gentleman's dish, and my mother saw her future laid out on the linen cloth. Over her body, he confessed the error. Only a gentleman in tales forgives an assailant. The daughter a gift to absolve and assuage.

And so I had gone to sea. Though from the cool of the patio I returned to my garret, where some days passed, and I felt a cooling of my remaining passions.

Word followed of my father's illness. Distance covered by boat and train, and finally I found myself again in Budapest, by the side of death. Together we confessed our various parts, loudly and over the voice of the other.

What good can come of looking into the futures of others? he asked me. Sometimes, in the rising steam of a stock pot, I spot a slim curving light, and suspect that happiness still awaits me. However, such harbingers are so rarely applicable.

In the procession of black crepe from the house to the graveyard, below a striking veil, I looked forward, with some trepidation. Already, I had spent so much time in discovery of the past. In Barcelona a home awaited, a mother's home, and a mother's lover, but the site of sorrow, such bitter herbs. There the sad carpet unrolled and stretched for many years across several borders. In Budapest I had a father's home I had left on my own so long ago. Why not return to the trail of the circus? Would I always wander, homeless?

I wander for a time in grief. In Perpignan, I arranged to meet an elderly chef of great renown. In the bottom of her house, she kept a kitchen with an open fire in a great copper dome. Every surface was covered in Marseille tiles in green and gold. She presented her wisdoms:

A well-tossed salad holds as much flavor on its leaves as clings to the bowl.

Pack the coffee pot tightly, and await the dark brew.

With great force, cut cleanly through the stalks of woody herbs.

Asparagus, below the ground, grows pale and thick and fibrous.

Carême said: Grandeur, perfection, inside and out, in servitude.

Carême said: Attention please to the scaffolding of dough and preserved fruits.

Alas, disjoint the fowl. Disjoint the joint of meat.

If butter is pressed into an earthen bell, it stays cool enough in a well of cold water.

Direct flame to char the skins of tomatoes, to char the pepper, to blacken the toast.

Into the pot, the screaming crustacean.

Out of the saucepan, the caramel forms shapes while cooling in the pan of snow.

Never a dog under foot.

A spoon in the glass carafe takes in the heat of boiling water.

Dumas Père said: First the egg, then the vinegar. Bouillon to quell the insurrection.

Dumas Père said: I'll send you your salad by messenger.

A yolk runs across the clean white china.

Beware the gray steak.

Even as she spoke, I saw her death in a cloud of flour rising up from a paper bag.

Where I walk, illness follows. I continued, exhausted, on to the next town.

In Marseille, on the Canebière, I heard the carillon. Again, I found my circus. The trapeze artist was nowhere to be found. In the story-teller's tent, I discovered his fate. Injured after a fall, he limped back to the family kilns in a village where for generations everyone had been a potter. A century of heavy platters, deep, ridged bowls, and goblets in glazed clay, all decorated with curving trout, in gold and gray.

Once, I told the story-teller, a Hungarian sailor fell in love with a Spanish gypsy, who was already a bride. And so…I continued…until father and daughter roamed the earth as ghosts, or gypsies.

I made some necessary changes, but kept the legend intact.

How lucky, she said. So sensational, and so moral. She noted the changes on a bright, clean sheaf.

I dream of the gypsies, but now must stay still. Onward, toward Vallauris, and the fluted plate, with its trout in profile, so that to eat a fish is to discover a fish.

—∾—

The Tartan Detective

I.

Inside this house, a precipice. The vacation repeats itself: the flight arrives late. Stationed in the inn, light breaks through the pale slatted blinds of the bedroom, carefully tucked into eyelet and down. I emerge from the shadowed corner in blonde wig and dark glasses, knee boots, belted trench coat. Onward the surveillance outing! Paces between houses, retraced. A graying bent head viewed through the window. This familiar neighborhood sorts into shapes, brick boxes, shingled apse, a pencil addition, eraser cones. Is it evening? I circle the block. The capitulation begins. Next, five carefully demarcated days noted in the moleskine. I transfer the bags to the next location.

(The seams of her stockings are perfectly aligned, her legs charming inside them. She crosses the tiles to a cocktail lounge where her father is seated on a cylindrical stool. In lieu, she has come to ask for her own hand. Her hat in leopard print sits oddly to one side, as though glued in place. There is something not quite right about her face. The soup has gone cold. Her diamond is blinding—the light comes off in lines inside a haze. The band begins a monotonous refrain. He will see her off at the platform.)

In the yard, an ornamental canon, stationary, snow-covered. Snow falls on the outside pane of the Victorian. Inside, embers litter the hearth. Milo naps just out of reach through the glass. His head falls forward into a paperback novel. Alone for now. I slip off into the night when a man selling bread joins me on the porch. The doorbell rings, and within the house the scene shifts. I circle the block and drop a match in the gutter. Night comes with a staggering cold wind. Days continue, passed in the library of the guesthouse, where the books sit perfectly still.

(Under a tartan blanket, the train is just now passing. Already, the itinerary has been set with every hour accounted. The boat awaits. Who could guess so much time could pass with only water in between? How carefully she has been incorporated. The exchange is between men, and the pass-off easily executed. It argues that somewhere, from within the elusive mists of his mountains, on his island, a mechanical arm cranks the machine into motion. Still, at the end of every steamer plank awaits a delectable male, though, on occasion, beyond and lingering in the distance.)

This town wavers in the light, as though cut from silk. Still, it has an everyday quality: ready-made. Today, I strike out in a different direction and wander along a street of barbershops. The tavern keeper affects an accent. The small beer garden opens with a gate onto the back alley and the dumpsters. Empty, with ice on the flagstones. Wrought iron chairs leant against their tables. In the moleskine, I tip in two maps. Lightning flashes in the snow clouds to the west. Point of departure noted. When I've located a quarter, I locate the payphone. Milo answers, brightly. I speak in an even voice, with grouped words, and cast around a vague eye. The beer garden fills with thick pigeons.

I swallow my last page of orders, written in a mysterious hand. We are often unknown to our betters; in this case, our leaders remain hidden, for their own safety, disguised, figures in a haze.

(His furlough begins a silhouette within the fog. In his naval costume he is entirely removed. An outcropping of curls, very grand epaulets, he is an unlikely tourist. He takes a turn on the pier, and so they fall in step in a similar direction, without introduction. The mists obscure the water's edge and the island beyond. The boat is rinsed in salt water, and upturned on the quay. There is no hope of an outing. Following on tradition, the men deliver a few pointed phrases, their demeanor quick and accepting.

In the background, the narrow tower of a castle opens up on one side, a cutaway. The curse is prominently displayed. Above the wave's measured break, the baying shanty of seals rises. They love the warm, balmy weather.)

The west deck of the inn faces the mountains, close to the clouds. Gray in all directions. The guests lounge under lap-robes, invalided. The weather is coldest here just before spring. I zip in my plaid lining.

A decadent sky-rise blocks the view of the Victorian through field glasses. I copy down the transcribed notes: cipher. It begins: The former man sought the pluribus eagle, but went mad.

On given harsh mornings, I awake from a dream where I've been waltzing with a torch. The air is clouded with bees en route to their next location. In the dream, I can never recall if I am the pursued or the pursuer, or if, as I suspect, the role alternates.

For days, I trace the streets. I cable. No instructions. I follow the steps back to the Victorian. A pungent boxwood splits through the gapping boards of the porch. The door stands agape; the staircase curls blackly toward the upstairs offices. I wait in the dark of the parlor, though hear no footsteps on the landing. From a stained glass dormer high up in the stairwell, a ruddy spot of light crosses the banister and strikes the landing carpet. The office above is ransacked, disarray. Papers blanket the floor and chairs, and float in the corner cobweb. An invitation, carelessly discarded, in Milo's hand. I borrow the car.

(She's a guest, but he's a family friend. Hare for supper. She notes the face in umbrage, which moves into the light of a manor's corner window in the perpendicular wing. He stretches long to urge an indiscretion. Shadow rests in the gap. The apple of his cheeks, in lines and gashes. Nevertheless, she manages some sleep. The fog continues, unremitting.

In the morning they telephone from below the waterfall to secure any vacancy. The day escapes undocumented, but very much in company. That night, she wilts into a silk pajama set. The sea wind picks up the floral curtains. The lamplight forms a rosette on the ceiling above her face in the camber of smoke. The nightly prayer gathers steam. She begins to count the beams, and as the wind blows off the mist, the island can now be seen.)

The standard skids lightly along the mountain road. The ski lodge, in cedar hues, juts over the lake; the green face of the water extends it beyond the seam of beach. On the opposite shore, I pry open a fishing shanty. I strike a match on a canvas sail. Across the water, a wedding procession moves onto the frozen lawn for photographs. I follow the bride with field glasses. A window in the highest corner of the lodge flashes obliquely. The scullery installed not in the basement but in the attic! I recognize Milo's apron in dark stripes. The jig is up! Spotted from a great distance, through the glass. From the dock I signal: bravo, yankee, bravo, yankee, echo. Still, he motions me over the lake. Dark comes on across the water; last light behind the range. I cross on a bar of ice without difficulty.

In the lobby, duffers clutter the fire pit. The elevator is empty, but with the top floor button already depressed. It clambers skyward, and opens onto a long slatted corridor. Overhead, a skylight shines blackly, broken with stars. His condo is all kitchen. Milo waits below the pine garland, fingers warm from skinning charred fruit.

(The war continues in grim distant tones. A radiogram carries instructions from across the water, but the boat will not travel. The night passes again below beams. She slips out before dawn while the girl polishes the stones of the hotel's foyer. Now out of uniform, done up in plaids and cables, Torquil breakfasts behind glass. From the scrap of her note, he follows from manor to manor, along the coast. The properties have been let, or taken by the RAF, who generously will do it all up again as originally found. Destitute gentry curl deep into their tweeds. In 400 rooms, and 400 portraits, there is only warmth in the linen closet, against the boiler's copper pipes.)

Safely inside the lodge scullery, I finally throw off my disguise, where below I'm blonde with dark sockets. For weeks, I've kept watch through the night. Overhead, the beams intersect, and the ceiling is paneled as in the quarters of a ship. The heels of my boots ring against the tiles. A banquet table is laid with a cloth and a carefully dressed hare.

His gesture is stock but effective, and from then on I move silently and keep my breath hushed. A listening mechanism concealed in a potted fern! He darkens the room. Beyond the picture window, the mountain face glows: carelessly near to us. For days the mountains have shown me which way is west, though now, they surround us.

A furtive embrace, and his kiss misses my mouth. Oh, Milo, who to trust? My coat falls open to vibrant effect. The tartan reveals itself. We begin the effortless movement of arms and legs, momentarily full and occupied. There is the smell of perfume, briefly, before I crumple under the cosh.

(Well, well my dears. She arrives in the company of dull pedants, and a grim young family of renters. One breezy tower is kept in-family, and so the legends are still recounted in the late afternoon by the grande dame. In filibeg, with quick step, he approaches with the tea, along a long corridor lit by dormers. Here, Torquil the displaced laird, the namesake of a golden eagle, narrows on his quarry. A hand of bridge begins across the long table. Who will make a fourth? The littlest girl reads coolly from a book of fairies. The two principals exit, having no knowledge of the game.

Little remains of the furlough week meant to be passed in distant quarters on the small island. For her, tomorrow, the island, at all cost! Tonight, on this dour property, the pipers begin a wedding dance high in the loft of the stables, where this frame gives only the view of moving feet at the crest of the ladder's rise. Once she takes the first rung, the way back down is blocked in arms.)

Many hours later, I retrieve myself, roughly, from the slats. A now rising dark above my dark socket, and the room partitions to shadows and haze. I search the perimeters. An upturned bedside table scatters the contents of his overnight case: a canister of toothpowder, a camera, a neckerchief monographed M— a postcard with pinked edges shows a line of mounted horsemen— and a page of sonata, but whose? What possible clues can these be? An impenetrable set. In a quick gust the balcony's French doors give way. Far below, troubadours serenade the honeymooning couple. I put on the flickering lamp and slip onto the narrow band of the balcony aglow with the clear sheen of the moon on the water. Restoring my wig and now his neckerchief, I move toward the threshold and set the blinds to half-mast. In the distance, beyond the water, the shadows gather to observe. It is impossible to say which among them takes Milo's shape, so clumped and hulking are these figures on the coveted shore.

Is there still the pale hope to unknot the bind? Again, I count out the factors, moving across the horizon, now, with bright allure. Forever vulnerable to the seduction of cool fingers and warning hands which announce, as though inked: Fictitious! This way does not go through to action. My dear Milo tosses me to the lions, or drugged, dragged, goes freely into their mouths. Oh, my Milo.

(If the whirlpool has begun and the boat moves in ever narrowing circles toward the eye, what now, when prayers go unanswered? There are three of them in the boat for the island. Torquil mans the rudder, his pipe bowl turned down against the spray. The engine is flooded, and the pilot passes into a trance. The legend recounts that the rope made from the hair of faithful maidens holds quick in the whorl. But girls fall in love so freely.

As in a dream of the island, it can't be reached, so with the sea, where she wants to go swimming, a week's vacation cannot foster so dangerous an adventure. The gale continues and each knot closer they are another knot off course. Into the swirl the boat tips steeply. The curtain of a wave cuts over the boat's edge between her person and pale gold Torquil. A coming storm, now smoke from kerosene lit under the caul of his slicker. A skin apart.)

What follows is an appraisal with no object. Only belligerent evergreens. With field glasses, I perform the surveillance. Circling dark forces creep along in the undergrowth. I drop from the balcony along knotted sheets, and then keep a footpath just adjacent to the bar of light running from the terrace's French doors to the edge of the lake. The wedding celebration runs long inside the lodge, where the waltzing couples divide and rejoin, and divide twice over. Alone or many, wakeful or dreaming? I furrow, and halt at the water's edge where, on the adjacent shore, a torch flickers. A haze behind my eyes floats fore and aft and I waft. From within the seam of my lining I draw the missive. In the light of the party these dispatch ravings fall forward in an image of speech, which I harden myself against: *Only when dead concern yourself with the accessories of death. All our resources dissipate, and results are few. A fog hangs over our paths from the cloud at the height of your head which smothers without notice. Forward we grind toward change: make use of the piercing clarity, or be left behind.*

A sound above in the clouds. The weather offers its enigmatic service. I fall again into a black pool and work my eyes toward stars, circling, in a thinning patch closed in by clouds. Water steals up, lapping at my hand, and like a turkey if I open my mouth I will drown in the coming torrents. Mouth, you are needed to decide things. Dear Milo, I am susceptible to grave rhetoric. The revolt will marry us or there will be mourning.

(In the battle of men against the sea it is not the sea which initiates. The circle of the pool draws the boat evenly from the shore of the island and from the shore of the mainland, and it is as if the boat, caught however briefly in the perimeter of the whorl, might shoot off in any direction, as a rock from a sling, and so decide. It is the engine which catches finally, where rope, however faithful, would have found no grip to anchor. In short of her eyes, Torquil recedes within the curve of water which divides them, and so seeks the calm below the surface, or the quiet eye. Water needs an inhabitant.

Sweet boy, brought up in the sea and grown old enough to desire and be desired. Caught on his belly on the rim of the boat, his legs tangle, and hold below the caul. So many unrequited loves end in just this way: the body draped half within, half without. His arms reach around the sea, but the sea is not a body to be grasped.)

II.

After some hours I awake on bare cobbled ground with the sun now risen. Gone from the lake, but still on the edge of water, a mill lade, and above me a village of birds quivering on a stone dovecot. I dip Milo's kerchief in the cool of the lade, and bathe my eyes, but regard all through an aura, watery and undulating.

From the deck of the mill, I slip onto the roof. The sun comes so strongly, I gain an anxious thirst before, again, I pass into sleep, soon again waking. But my hip seems stricken with palsy for a time. The day breaks apart in short lapses viewed through crystal. Soon the apparition of Milo bows over me, and, with evening hands, addresses my fever. A column of spark and ardor extends from my throat, through my mouth. My breath lifts the monogrammed silk.

A gap in the parapet shows the panorama: far away there is the blue line of what looks like the sea. West as I was? Do I walk without my knowledge, or have I been removed? I check my person. The moleskine unscathed! I examine the maps. I turn the book once, and again. At the summit of a small moor, crowning a plateau, a copse gives onto a hollow, a circle of confiding thicket and a flat green within, hidden completely from all but the bird's eye. An aerodrome! I am again in the thick of the enemy. The day draws long, and the plane is late, the gloaming far advanced, but I mark it. I awake in the lee of a stone. Ahead is the peaty bog, where soon I scuttle in bracken and heather.

Beyond the aerodrome's fixed thicket, the sky inverts. I hang thus above the clouds held to an indolent ground or—deepest within, farthest from outside—to Milo where I dangle the whole weight of my desire. Below, the abyss of sky. Sunstroke. The coming bloom. A great distance from the first lodge, I am on for the next, to reassemble and re-group.

(This boat does not go to the island. Instead they are returned to the quay, where the sleeping pilot is lifted into a shed. Inside the manor, they part quietly on the stairs. Torquil collapses at the fireside, in slicker and wet socks, his toes in the air. His sleep is brief, and in the night he awakes to the sound of calm. Out of the house he sits on the hill, island-side, and sees, for the first time this week, a view un-obstructed by fog or spray. The rich dark calm of the waters below. The quay looks roughened, battered, its shape sup-planted and effaced, where the water attempts to soften it. Night is a substance, also. It commingles so totally that a bit of night remains in the waters at dawn on this the last day of his furlough.

The white flash of silk adrift in the distance. What he knows about women is not much. At best, he hopes, a woman is a valve which would open.)

I travel the foothills, and lose myself in this way for a time, seeking the camp of our ally shipbuilders, whose location is starred on my map, though my own location remains unrecognized. I consult the moleskine, which gratefully remains, and take up the fountain pen with eagle's beak (a lady's pen) so that, now, the pen point extends the memory! A camera, a postcard, a page of music. The copper pots strung along the mantel in the lodge scullery. The father's portrait, in naval costume, on the mantelpiece: his absence unexplained. Milo, once our comrade, is now the suspect in an era of suspicion. I record the scraps. Impetuous, I write, and I doubt it, in margins, encrypted as in the journal of a child.

Herein, on the dark scrawled pages of the moleskine, I retrace the mission which so divides us. Overhead a plane circles, while I cower in the scrub's shadow. The account in code builds, and so with it offers my past and present, coming now quickly in ink from the mouth of the eagle. And again the recording of the last dispatch: *note this age which with its love of gluttony feeds the prosperity of brigands and traitors. Non-persons. Harvesters. Will the same machinery which propels their cause break them in its own implosion? Such naïve altruism is fatal. It is for us to cut off the fuel at its source.*

Naps between words. A vision begins, and Milo holds my shoulders on his lap. In locked regard, between us the cord tightens. Milo's hand dips into my chest, as through the meniscus, and gathers. It is a wakeful dream, far too thrilling to invite sleep. Why not linger in this dream? A dream which listens finally to the cacophony of the sensual?

Ominously, the voice of my dispatcher reminds me of the finger that points away from the body, and so attraction and desire pull us from our center. This lie I will never accept. Between action and reverie two paths stretch out, traversable but cordoned. The sides of this conflict remain rigid, though between us, myself and Milo, something else. Fraternity? A searing penetration?

A gap in the Dutch door lets out a slice of light, and a morsel of voice. I awake on the porch of the enemy encampment, where in camera, in closed meeting, a conference takes place. On the door a wreath of lemons blooms fruit.

(The day begins clear. On the piano's bench, he sits in uniform, chin in hand. What is seen out the window is little more than the flashing signal from a launch approaching the quay. Her spirits are considerably brightened. There are words on parting but no comment. The exchange moves across torpid hands, cool from the morning. With no furlough left, he forfeits the island.

The mountain has slipped a little or the swarming dust obscures the path toward town. He walks into the hills away from the edge of the sea. In melancholic reverie and watching the falconer whose uplifted glove awaits his returning messenger.)

Through the door's horizon break, only a thin interior slice is visible, wherein strange voices rise from false beards calling each other by the letters of the alphabet. A's dark scarf, B's dark glasses, C's tipped hat, D's raised collar. Several sets of hands, with only two voices. They prepare a course of assassination. A weapon concealed in the telephoto lens. The passage by sea plane. All this I learn, at the door of the enemy, to which I have been led or taken in search of Milo.

For some minutes my mind has trouble shaping things. How many days now wandering, and no clear origin? *We find our places in the conflict of the cause, displaced as we are in the world, saddened and crippled. Where artifice has overtaken our lips and eyes, our cheeks, the lines of the brow, now we spend ourselves, we strip ourselves bare,* quoth the dispatch.

A man without faults is still water. A man without faults is a man without facets, and is of little interest. I slip along the foundation. There is no sign of him anywhere in the compound. Already the scent of salt in the air reports the closeness of the sea. Tomorrow the shipbuilders at all cost, and will I reveal my secret?

(Into the castle, which he has never entered, to photograph the plaque whose grave warnings will make him victim. The staircase exposed to the air threads the layers of the crumbling tower, up toward the parapet, vined with green, down to the cellar, the well, and the crypt, where two ill-fated lovers were lashed together to a rock, ardently embraced in its moss.

The castle's exposure offers a vista, on one side the mountains, to the other the sea. From behind the black of the camera's shutter, his eye sits patiently. He considers the manacles and the water rising on the stone. In the right company, the lashing invites. It was from the top of the ladder that the dance began, the folk song confessed: there is only one girl for the soldier on leave.)

Safe among the shipbuilders, the weeks pass quietly at the edge of the sea, where my name remains hidden but my reputation renowned. In time the fever lifts, and with it the taste of Milo's lips, and the pressure of his hands, but not the lingering dark where the hand has once gripped me. Again, I wander carefully on the edge of men, barefoot along the rocks of the shore which cuts sharply apart, as the teeth of cliffs rise up from the water. In these narrow inlets the great skeletons of ships are lashed on stilts and slides.

Instructions follow with some reservations. Reluctantly I forward the moleskine, the last artifact of my tepid allegiance, or rather, my unyielding fidelity to all parties in question, equally, consistently. Note again the rhetoric of the dispatch, for indeed I too was once a reproachful lady-in-waiting. Evaded by Milo, I am returned to watching, where now by night, on the edge of the shore, I await the lights of the seaplane and the delivery of the chief, who any day must visit our outpost. The seaplane gives out men, and takes them up again, and I am the boatman between.

In an inn kept in-company, the rooms adjoin. In time I find myself in the bed of a ginger-headed shipwright whose pledging eyes are my equal. With each evening, I know already what he will answer softly, when much later I am looking in his face. When, in tangled shadows, he reveals what has already been on display. So begins this robust, wanton distraction. An unaccented ardor.

If an explanation is required, it should suffice that with certain girls passion moves as a wave over the ledge of a cliff, to return to sea again only in part. In the pool of the rock, the remainder holds still, and reflects.

(The pipers on the road repeat the tune. She approaches with quickstep at the head of the small procession. As he leaves the castle, the curse is revealed, so that together they begin to cross the glebe, where the meadow begins the hills.

The launch returns empty across the water which rests after the gale. How quiet it seems on the island. A reminder that the destination is rarely the terminus.)

A propeller on the horizon line.

Like the scholar who hides behind the books in his glass carrel, I withdraw myself inwardly from the cause, though, as ever, watched and watching. But who has the right to cloister themselves in an arrangement entirely of their own choosing? Await the dispatch. Prepare the boat. Deliver the passengers.

In the legend of the river of the dead, we awaken at night to knocking on the door. Strange boats line the shore, without passengers or navigators but heavily loaded and nearly sinking, their gunwales scarcely above the surface of the water. An hour's trip may take the entire night. The seaman's wisdom holds: never board an unknown boat.

I return to something I scarcely recall, daily life around the table.

The innkeeper awakens me with the signed dispatch. The signature in facsimile. I recognize the hand. I shove into the night waters and make for the seaplane. The lantern signals. In cloak and dark glasses, false beard and tipped hat, the chief crouches on the pontoon, soaked to his knees, timorous, clutching, and anticipating passage to the shore. If a car awaits him, we have only this short trip, but the weight of his body lies heavily in the prow. Broad shoulder, whose chill I know all too well, wedged in the point of my skiff! If we have not been introduced, it is for good reason.

Below his disguise I undress him to reveal the wound in his side, to which, until now, only the camera has been witness. I have heard it said that in our vocation a man's life is ancillary to his wanderings, variant excursions and forays, and so if one is afield, the other is adrift. Strike out from a point, trace the streets, retrace the steps, a hope to return to the point of origin. What of a girl's work? To mime the part is to be indistinguishable, even hallucinatory. Whatever happens now in Milo's dreams cannot be reported, and I, for one, have never had the courage to hope to report to him.

In place of Milo, an unending search for Milo. In place of Milo, the figure of dispatch.

And now the final piece: in a postcard where the wealth is in the stamp and for a page of music when a tune tells the story, all the clues are self-obscuring, and the dispatch only reverses the gaze. For now, on the side of Milo's overcoat, blood blooms blackly across the wool. He reclines into my boat, exhausted, resting in stretches. I see him sleeping, as wakefully, I tend the oars.

—⚬—

Acknowledgments

Thanks to the editors of the publications in which the following stories first appeared:

American Letters and Commentary: portions of "Ghosts and Lovers";
Conjunctions: "The Black Cat," "Light Carried on Air Moves Less";
Double Room: "The Actor at Dinner";
Encyclopedia A-E: "Entertainment";
Harp and Altar: "Seascape";
Highway 14: "What Was There Was Gone, Burning";
Lake Effect: "Exchange," "Russian Doll";
Salt Hill: "In Guffy's Plum Cricket";
Snowvigate: "She Came from the East";
Tarpaulin Sky: "Captive Girl for Cobbled Horsemen";
Unsaid: "The Scent of Apples" and "The Tartan Detective."

"Captive Girl for Cobbled Horsemen" is a study after a painting by Nancy Kiefer. "The Tartan Detective" is for Rene Char, or specifically for his code name, Alexandre. "Ghosts and Lovers" is for Robert Urquhart.

Finally, I would like to thank Rikki Ducornet, Robert Urquhart, Thalia Field, Brian Evenson, Brian Kiteley, Penelope Creeley, Laird Hunt and Keith and Rosmarie Waldrop for their friendship, mentorship, and general wisdom. Also, many thanks to Forrest Gander, C.D. Wright, Rebecca Brown, and Anne Waldman for their advice and support.

—m—

About the Author

Joanna Howard is the author of *In the Colorless Round,* a chapbook with artwork by Rikki Ducornet (Noemi Press). Her work has appeared in *Conjunctions, Chicago Review, Unsaid, Quarterly West, American Letters & Commentary, Fourteen Hills, Western Humanities Review, Salt Hill, Tarpaulin Sky* and elsewhere. Her stories have been anthologized in *PP/FF: An Anthology, Writing Online,* and *New Standards: The First Decade of Fiction at Fourteen Hills.* She has also co-translated, with Brian Evenson, *Walls* by Marcel Cohen (Black Square, 2009). She lives in Providence, Rhode Island and teaches at Brown University.

BOA Editions, Ltd.
American Reader Series

—m—

Colophon

On the Winding Stair, by Joanna Howard is set in Adobe Garamond Pro which is based on roman types cut by Jean Jannon in 1615. Jannon followed the designs of Claude Garamond which had been cut in the previous century.

—◦◦◦—

The publication of this book is made possible, in part, by the following individuals:

Anonymous

Alan & Nancy Cameros ◦◦◦ Gwen & Gary Conners

Peter & Suzanne Durant ◦◦◦ Pete & Bev French

Judy & Dane Gordon ◦◦◦ Kip & Debby Hale

Bob & Willy Hursh ◦◦◦ Peter & Robin Hursh

Nora A. Jones ◦◦◦ X. J. & Dorothy M. Kennedy

Jack & Gail Langerak ◦◦◦ Rosemary & Lewis Lloyd

John Edward Lovenheim & Barbara
Pitlick Lovenheim Charitable Trust

Steven O. Russell & Phyllis Rifkin-Russell

Vicki & Richard Schwartz

Dan & Nan Westervelt, in honor of
Patricia Braus & Edward Lopez

Pat & Mike Wilder ◦◦◦ Glenn & Helen William

—◦◦◦—